The Tritium Hypothesis

Nicolle Morock

Acknowledgments

Thank you to my family and friends who are a constant source of inspiration and encouragement and who put up with me talking about "the book I need to finish writing" for longer than I care to admit. I offer a special thank you to Gayle, Carol, and Elizabeth for proofreading this one. Your eye for spelling, grammar, typos, confusing sentences, and clarification was exactly what I needed to finally finish Tritium. Nathan, you have my gratitude for designing a cool cover for what I hope everyone will consider a fun story.

Chapter 1

The forest ranger squinted his blue eyes against the late afternoon sun in an effort to scan the bright sky for the source of the hum. There was nothing to see, at least nothing out of the ordinary. That hum, though, was not ordinary. In fact there was something other-worldly to it when it started softly and appeared to get louder as if something was approaching. There was a mechanical tinge to it that grated on his nerves like nails on a chalkboard and made his eyes water. He thought to himself that maybe *whir* was a better description. Just as quickly as the sound arrived, it faded away leaving no clue to its origin.

Fifteen-year-old Shana Lovell was helping her mother prepare the picnic table behind their two story farmhouse for a nice dinner outside. It was too beautiful of an afternoon to stay indoors. "Mom, do you hear that?" Shana asked as she set a place for her father.

Sylvia paused to listen. There was a faint hum coming from the woods several hundred feet behind the house. "Yeah, I do. Wonder what it is."

The hum grew a bit louder as the source was drawing closer. Both women were looking towards the trees. Suddenly, there was the crackling of breaking branches - lots of branches - then a loud *thud*.

"Tim?" Sylvia called. She turned to see her husband flying through the back door with his shotgun in hand.

"What the hell was that?" He asked.

"Don't know," Sylvia answered. "It came from the woods."

Shana was still staring toward the trees. "I think it was above the woods."

Tim Lovell ran across the field toward the forest.

"Be careful!" Sylvia yelled.

"That's what I want on my tombstone," Rayna spoke into the cell phone cradled between her right ear and her shoulder with her brown curls crushed between them. Her hands were busy picking up Cloud, her sleek, black, green-eyed cat.

"Excuse me?" Dawn asked from the other end of the line.

"Yeah, that's perfect. 'She died trying.'"

"And you want that on your tombstone?"

"Why not? People always say, 'I'm going to do this or die trying,' or 'you never fail until you stop trying.' So, I want it to say that I didn't fail."

"But if you died trying, then you stopped trying by virtue of dying. So you want your tombstone to say you failed?" Rayna's sister always had an argument against anything unusual that Rayna wanted to do.

"That's not what I meant!"

"You might want to rethink that. Why are we having this discussion anyway? Are you dying?"

"No."

"Then why be so morbid?"

"Tombstones aren't morbid. You need to know these things." Rayna stated matter-of-factly.

"Tell Mom, not me."

"Mom won't care. We're supposed to outlive our parents, you know."

"Uh-huh. Speaking of Mom," Dawn changed the subject, "you need to call her."

"I can't today."

"Why not?"

Rayna could hardly hear her sister over Cloud's loud purring. "Every time I talk to Mom she gives me PMS!"

"What? How?"

"PMS... Please Marry Somebody! She wants more grandbabies, and you told her you were done providing them, thank you very much!"

"You're welcome," Dawn ignored the sarcasm in Rayna's voice. "I gave you two nephews and a niece, you know. My work is done."

"So the pressure's on me now to get married and have babies."

"Don't worry about it."

"That's easy for you to say. You got married at twenty-four and wasted no time. Apparently, I've done nothing but waste time as far as Mom's concerned."

"She'll get over it."

"Right. Sure." Rayna's phone beeped. "Someone's on the other line."

"OK. I'll talk with you tomorrow."

"Ta-ta for now!" Rayna glanced at her cell phone as she hit the button to change calls. "Hi, Barb, what's up?"

As Rayna's little red pickup truck cruised up the long, sloping driveway of the Lovell farm, she took in the picturesque scene. On each side of the driveway, horses stood in lush green grass. Beyond the curve in the drive, Rayna could see the Victorian house welcoming her visit. She had always dreamed of living on a horse farm like this one.

Rayna parked the truck behind the sheriff's car, and reality broke her daydream. On the porch, the sheriff and a deputy were finishing up their note taking. A man and woman in their forties stood speaking to the sheriff while a teenage girl sat on a porch swing about ten feet away from them.

Sheriff Dean Sutton, a tall, broad-shouldered, middle-aged man turned his attention from Tim and Sylvia Lovell toward Rayna at the sound of her truck door closing. "Well, Rayna Smith, what brings you out this way?"

Rayna was sure he knew the answer to his own question. "Two phone calls and some curiosity."

"You know what they say about curiosity." He glanced at his deputy and turned his attention back toward the concerned Lovells. Without looking at Rayna again, he added, "Fieldman and Jenkins are around back."

"Thanks." Rayna said and gave a polite little wave to Sylvia and Tim.

"Is that..." Sylvia asked the sheriff pointing at Rayna as she walked toward the back yard.

"Yes, ma'am." He answered. "I just have a few more questions for you before we leave you to your other guests."

As Rayna rounded the back corner of the house, she looked up at the sky above the trees. Being a meteorologist, looking at the sky was as reflexive as swallowing, but there was something unusual above the tree line that caught her attention immediately. Floating on the wind currents and circling over a fixed location were what seemed to be hundreds of buzzards. It was as if they were pointing the way to the reason she had been called that afternoon.

When she lowered her gaze to the backyard of the Lovell farm, she saw two familiar faces. Sam Jenkins had been one of Rayna's best buddies since high school. With a slightly round face and nice dimples, the average-height black man always had a smile for Rayna even when the situation didn't warrant one. James Fieldman was a bit shorter than Rayna. She noticed as she drew closer to the two men that Fieldman's hair was becoming more salt than pepper. His blue eyes were still piercing, but nothing else about the man ever really stood out to her.

"Hi, guys!" Rayna said to her two friends.

"Hey, Sweetie," Sam always greeted Rayna with a bear hug.

"Rayna," Fieldman was a bit more reserved and always to the point, "thanks for coming on such short notice."

"Do we ever get much notice on cases like these? I mean... not that we've ever had one quite like this." Rayna said.

"This one takes the cake!" Sam exclaimed. "Rayna, you gotta see this!"

Rayna took a deep breath to steel her nerves and answered, "Yeah. I guess I do. You don't have to lead the way, though." She pointed to the buzzards circling above the trees behind the yard. "I suspect they're marking the spot pretty well."

The three crossed from the short grass into some taller grass and then into the woods. While they walked, Rayna asked how Fieldman's daughter was doing in college. It had been a while since they had spoken.

"Krista's doing fine," he answered. "She's starting her junior year at the end of the summer. She still loves geology, so I guess she chose the right major."

"Like father, like daughter, huh?" Sam asked.

"Yep. I was afraid I had pushed her into it, but her mother and I really tried to be as hands off on the subject as possible."

"So, is she going to be our next MUFON contact when she graduates?" Rayna asked.

"I doubt it. She's not a replica of me. She's talking about working for the state or the USGS. Besides, I'm not ready to retire from all of this so soon." Fieldman waved his hands in the direction of the little clearing in the woods that they were approaching.

Rayna took another deep breath and decided that was not a good idea. "Ew!" She held her shirtsleeve to her nose. "I hadn't thought about the smell." Despite the odor, she did what she could to prepare herself for what they were about to see. She hated violence. She loved horses. This was going to be tough.

In the clearing, they found the carcass of a dead horse to accompany the increasing stench. The animals jaw was missing as well as part of the mane and an eye. The rear end appeared to have been cored out. What was worse was the way the horse was situated on the ground. It was in a messy, broken heap, as if it had been dropped there by some unseen, gigantic hand.

Rayna again looked up to the sky. The buzzards continued to circle above the trees directly overhead. Then she noticed something else. The tree limbs directly above them had been broken – all of them, all the way up to the sky. Rayna lowered her eyes to the ground and saw large limbs scattered about them everywhere. Happy for the diversion away from the poor, deceased animal, she walked over to the closest limb to examine it.

The limb was fresh and looked as if it had been torn from the tree in an abrupt, violent struggle. It was obvious which side had been closest to the ground by the shape of the broken edge. Rayna stood up and glanced around her at the rest of the fallen branches. They all looked similar. Only their sizes varied.

"Crazy." She whispered to herself.

"Rayna! Over here." Fieldman was standing over the carcass with a piece of brightly colored floral fabric over his nose. Rayna noticed that Sam had a piece of the same fabric.

"Hey, where's mine?" she asked. "Sorry. The Lovell's daughter only gave us two. We didn't think to ask for an extra." Sam held his out for her to inspect. It looked like a fancy napkin. "She took 'em off the clothesline for us."

"They look good on you." Rayna smiled while trying not to gag on the smell. "I really can't stay back here too much longer. Did you notice anything else I should see?"

Fieldman answered, "Just that there are no flies and the birds up there are circling but staying well above the trees. They won't touch it."

"It will be interesting to see how long that lasts. They obviously know there's a kill of some sort down here." Sam added. "Fieldman brought some camera traps to set up out here tonight. We'll come back and see how it looks tomorrow."

"OK. Let me know. I'm assuming you've already photographed, measured, and taken notes on the scene." Rayna said.

Sam answered, "Yes, we did it as soon as the sheriff cleared it. The family requested that I don't put this in the paper, so my work here is strictly for the investigation. It's definitely newsworthy, but I'd rather respect their wishes as long as I can. Once my editor gets wind of it, that might have to change, though."

"You're a good man, Sam." Rayna gave him a hug and then patted Fieldman on the back. "James, I'll talk to you soon." Just as she turned to leave, Rayna's cell phone rang. "Hello?"

"Rayna?" It was Barb again. "I've got something new for you, but it might be related to everything else. I mean... I don't know."

"What is it?" Rayna asked.

"There's a forest ranger or park ranger or something... his name is Steven Wolf..."

"Did you say 'Wolf'?"

"Yeah, Steven Wolf. He called down here a little while ago and asked if anyone in the area had called in about a strange noise. He described it as something between a hum and a whir."

"What did you tell him?" Rayna asked.

"I told him that someone did report it and the sheriff is checking it out. I also gave him your name."

"What? Why?"

"He sounded cute." Barb answered. "I mean, come on! His name is 'Wolf'."

"He's probably some middle-aged, balding, guy with bad teeth."

"He's a ranger. I'm pretty sure they have dental insurance." Barb insisted.

Rayna laughed. "What else did you tell him?"

"That I'd have you meet him this evening at the diner in town."

"Barb!"

"No worries. He'll call when he gets there. Oh, yeah... I gave him your number, too."

"Woman! We need to talk!"

"Oops! I have another call coming in. I'm still at work. Bye!" With that, Barb hung up.

Chapter 2

It didn't take much for Rayna to convince Sam to go with her to meet a stranger at the diner in town. Sam was like the protective big brother that Rayna never had. While the idea itself of meeting a ranger didn't worry her, the idea of meeting a strange man after the day's events made her a little leery. Sam told her he didn't mind joining her. He was hungry anyway.

Their little town of Jupiter, Tennessee, sat in a valley in the Great Smokey Mountains. The picturesque setting hid the reality of a town struggling to survive. The sawmill and furniture factory closed the previous fall, and hundreds of blue-collar workers had to leave to find work elsewhere. Those that stayed were having a hard time making ends meet. The rest of the town's population considered themselves lucky or blessed and did what they could to help their less fortunate friends and family.

Sam and Rayna knew they were two of the lucky ones. Sam was a reporter for a paper in Chattanooga covering the eastern side of the state and focusing on life in the rural areas. Most of his work was done by telecommuting. Rayna had her own small business that kept her comfortable enough considering she lived alone with no husband or children to care for. Cloud was all she had, and that cat really seemed to be caring for Rayna instead of the other way around.

As the pair walked into the diner, they both scanned the room for a man in a ranger's uniform, but to no avail. The dark-haired waitress behind the counter gave a friendly smile. "Well, hello, Miss Rayna! How's your day goin'?"

"Pretty well, Gina, thanks." Rayna answered politely.

Gina leaned over the counter and motioned Rayna to come closer. "I'm not sure if you want to ask Mr. Sam to leave. Your blind date's sitting in the corner over there." She pointed to the man in the corner booth farthest from the door.

7

Rayna tried to look as discretely as possible in his direction but couldn't get a good look from her angle.

Sam on the other hand was staring. He pulled Rayna away from the counter by the back of her shirt. "Thanks, Gina. I'll be fine. You know... like a chaperone."

"Sure thing!" Gina answered. "I'll be over in a minute to take your orders."

"Chaperone?" Rayna whispered under her breath.

"Yep." Sam answered.

The man at the booth stood up, and Rayna thought she was going to fall over. Barb was right. He was cute. No. He was gorgeous.

Steven Wolf did his best to stand up when he saw Rayna and Sam approach his table. The attempt didn't work out so well since he was sitting at a booth and the table was in the way. He smiled anyway and held his hand out to Rayna from his crooked stance. "Hi, Rayna? I'm Steven Wolf." He gave her a nice firm handshake. Sam held his out as well, and the ranger took it. "Nice to meet you."

"Sam Jenkins." Sam introduced himself. "I'm an old friend and colleague of Rayna's."

"I'm Rayna," was all Rayna managed to squeak out. Her voice didn't want to work. She just wanted to take in the view. Steven Wolf was a little taller than Sam. Rayna guessed he was close to 6 feet. He had blue eyes that could only be described as mesmerizing and long dark hair held back in a ponytail. His skin was tan, and he did not look anything like the man she had pictured. Sam gave her a little nudge to get her to take her place in the booth, so he could sit down. She slid along the bench and sat across from the ranger, smiling stupidly.

Before Rayna could rein in her thoughts, Gina approached with two glasses of water in hand. She set them down in front of Sam and Rayna. "Thanks, Gina." Sam said.

"No problem." Gina answered. She looked at Rayna and Steven apparently locked in a staring match. "I'll just give you a moment to look at the menus," she said and walked back to the counter.

Steven didn't realize he was staring. All he knew was that the woman who used to do the weather on the 6 o'clock news was sitting across from him with a silly grin on her face. She was even cuter in person, but her hair was curly. He didn't expect that. She had curly, long brown hair and deep brown eyes. Those eyes were looking back at him. He was suddenly aware of his thoughts. "Um... sorry. I didn't mean to... I mean... what's good here?"

Sam answered, "I like the beef tips on rice."

Rayna managed to break her gaze and look down at the menu. She was sure that her face was turning red. It definitely felt hot. She shot a sideways glance at Sam who had a funny little smirk on his face. "Those are good. I'm partial to the BLT on wheat." Her voice was back. She took a sip of her ice water and tried to recompose herself. It wasn't like her to swoon over a man, and she wasn't sure how to handle it.

Sam hadn't seen Rayna react like that since high school. He thought no man could make her blush. "Miss Rayna," he started, imitating Gina "you always get the BLT. Try something new. New and exciting is a good thing, right Mr. Wolf?"

"You can just call me 'Wolf.' All my friends do."

"OK, Wolf," Gina was back. "What would you like to eat?"

"I'll take a BLT on wheat with chips," he answered while handing Gina the menu and smiling at Rayna.

All Rayna wanted to do was sink so low into her seat that she couldn't be seen. Of course, that didn't work. Gina wanted her order, too. "I'll... um... have the same."

Sam grabbed Rayna's menu and stacked it on his to hand over to Gina. He looked at Rayna and looked at Wolf and then said, "I'll have the Reuben." Rayna looked at him in amazement. "New and exciting, right?"

Gina giggled. "Yessir, an *exciting* Reuben. I'll see what we can do about that. Maybe some hot pepper sauce on the side?" She winked at Sam and walked away.

Rayna took a deep breath. "So, Mr. Wolf, Barb said you had something to share with us?"

"Please call me 'Wolf,'" he repeated. "I was on duty earlier this afternoon."

"On duty?" Sam asked.

"Yes, I'm a forest ranger. I was on duty up on Bell Mountain, about halfway up to be exact. I had stopped to move some debris off the road when I heard this sound. It wasn't normal. It was something between a hum and a whir. There was a metallic tinge to it. It was getting louder like it could be getting closer, but I never saw it. It started abruptly, but kind of faded out, after a few minutes. I didn't have a good feeling about it."

"So, it wasn't like a helicopter or a plane?" Sam asked.

"No. It sounded like it was coming from the sky, but it didn't sound like anything I've ever heard before. I tried to place it, but I couldn't."

Rayna asked, "Could it have been something on the ground echoing through the valley below, or even something on the mountain, but the sound was carrying in a weird way?"

Wolf gave a sigh. "I thought about that. I don't know. It didn't sound like anything I recognized. It really sounded like it was coming from above, not below. I just had a bad feeling. You know when your gut gets a little... turned upside down?"

Rayna knew that feeling well. "Yes, I know what you mean."

"How often do you go with your gut like that?" Sam questioned.

"I try to use logic first, but as a ranger, I have to trust my instinct. It's part of being in the wilderness."

"I understand." Rayna confirmed. "If you don't trust your gut, it nags at you until you start paying attention or until it's too late."

"I guess you must use your instinct when forecasting?" Wolf asked.

9

"I use it all the time. It's an integral part of my life." She answered.

"She's not lying." Sam said. "Rayna is more than just a pretty weather girl."

"Ugh. Sam…" Rayna started.

"Hush. I speak the truth." Sam interrupted. "Rayna, or Spooky as I like to call her, is one of the best paranormal investigators around. She uses her intuition and her scientific mind. She's a neat little hybrid."

"Intuition?" Wolf was intrigued. "So, are you a medium?"

Rayna rolled her eyes as Sam answered for her. "Yes."

"No." Rayna quickly corrected him. "I'm not comfortable with that title. I'm a sensitive."

"What's the difference?" Wolf asked.

"Semantics." Sam answered.

"Seriously, Sam, stop." Rayna glared at him. She hated having these conversations with strangers. "The difference is that there is a stigma and an expectation attached to the title 'medium' that I am not comfortable with. People hear 'medium' and expect me to be able to summon their dead loved ones or tell their fortunes or carry a crystal ball. I don't do that stuff."

Sam laughed quietly. "Her crystal ball is cracked. Hehehe."

Rayna glared at him again. He was really asking for trouble tonight. "Laugh it up, reporter boy." She turned her attention back to the ranger. "I never had a crystal ball."

Sam started to say something, but Gina was back with their meals stacked up on a tray. She set their plates in front of them. "Need anything else?"

"No, thanks." Rayna answered.

"Oh," Gina said pulling something out of her pocket. "Here you go, Mister Sam." She put a jar of Texas Pete in front of him. "Enjoy!"

When Gina was clear of hearing distance, Sam whispered, "Tarot cards, pendulums, dowsing rods, but she's not lying. She never had a crystal ball."

Wolf looked at Rayna, intrigued. "Oh, really? Then you are a fortune teller?"

"Only if you consider a weather forecast a fortune," she answered. "I don't use those things for that reason. I have the tarot because I was given the deck. I pull it out a few times a year when I can't quiet my mind enough to know a direction to take. They are a tool for listening to…" she waved her hands in the air around her, "God, or my angels, or my spirit guides or the universe. It's hard to explain. It depends on what you believe. I *do not* use them to read for other people."

"I never would have taken you for a paranormal investigator." Wolf said.

"Nobody does. She is full of surprises." Sam answered for Rayna.

Gina was back. "How's your food?" She asked.

"Yummy," answered Rayna.

"Miss Rayna, I forgot to tell you that my momma said 'hi,' and that she misses watching you on the news. That new girl, Rebecca what's-her-face, just isn't as good. She always gets it wrong."

Rayna blushed a little. "Well, Gina, you tell your momma that I said "hi" back and not to be too hard on Rebecca. Forecasting isn't always easy."

"Gee... you made it look easy." Gina said.

"I just knew how to wing it." Rayna smiled. "Rebecca's still pretty new at it. You have to give her time to get more comfortable. That's all."

"I guess." Gina walked back to the counter.

Rayna was thankful for an excuse to change the subject. "I hope you don't mind my saying, Mr. Wolf, but you don't look like a typical park ranger. I expected someone a little more... clean cut."

Wolf stroked his chin. Is my shadow showing?"

"No, that's not what I meant." Rayna couldn't see any sign of facial hair. "I meant... well... aren't rangers supposed to have short hair and look a bit more G.I.?"

"I guess most do," Wolf said. "I don't get much flack for the ponytail. I can claim cultural differences."

"Cultural?" Sam asked.

"I'm half-Native."

"Cherokee?" Rayna questioned.

"No. Chickasaw," Wolf answered.

"And the other half?" Rayna asked.

"Scotch-Irish."

"That explains the blue eyes." Sam observed knowing where Rayna was going with her thoughts. He'd known her long enough to know her type – long dark hair and blue eyes.

"And you?" Wolf asked Rayna.

Sam answered. "African-American."

"I think he was asking me, Sam," Rayna said. "I'm pretty sure your heritage is obvious."

"Well, you never know these days," Sam grinned.

Rayna answered Wolf, "I'm just a hybrid as Sam said. I'm Italian, English, and Dutch, with a little Native thrown in."

"Oh, really? Which tribe?" Wolf asked.

"My grandmother will tell you Mohican or Mohawk, but I'm pretty sure it's Esopus. She's more concerned with notoriety than actuality."

"So you're family is not from around here either?" Wolf asked.

"No. I mean yes. I mean that my immediate family is here, but my parents are from New York and Pennsylvania. So the extended family is there."

Sam interrupted, "Maybe we should get back to the task at hand. I've got to be leaving soon."

"Oh, yeah." Rayna agreed. "So what do you think we should do next, Sam?"

"As soon as we can get him, you and I will meet the professor back at the horse farm." Sam answered Rayna.

"Horse farm?" Wolf asked.

"We had a report similar to yours, but worse today at a farm south of here." Rayna explained. She was being cautious about giving too much detail. The family requested discretion.

"If it's not too much trouble," Wolf began, "I'd like for one or both of you to come with me to talk with someone who heard something similar on the outskirts of the park. Any insight you can give him would be helpful."

"Who?" Rayna asked.

"Mr. Don Hill," Wolf answered. "He's a bit of a hermit, but a nice man. He doesn't say much, so when he called me about a weird sound last week, I paid attention. I just didn't know what to tell him, so I told him that I'd get back to him about it. I still don't know what to tell him, but I feel like we should go talk with him. It might help you somehow, too."

Sam seemed uninterested for some reason, so Rayna spoke up. "I'll come with you." Out of the corner of her eye, she saw Sam smile.

"I'll let Rayna join you, Mr. Wolf. I have a few things to take care of this evening."

"Did you mean right now?" Rayna asked Wolf.

"If that's alright with you," he answered. "I know he's home. He's basically always home. I can just call him and let him know we're coming."

Don Hill's house sat a few hundred feet up the side of a mountain on a dirt road. It wasn't much to look at. In fact, it was the type of place a person might think was deserted. The windows were dark, but the porch light was on casting odd shadows in the peeling, green paint. As Wolf and Rayna exited Wolf's Jeep, Rayna realized there was a person sitting in one of the shadows on that porch. He was an elderly black man with an old mutt at his feet. The dog gave a little bark as Rayna and Wolf approached.

"Hush, Jax!" The old man said. "Ranger, it's nice to see ya out here."

"It's nice to see you, too, Mr. Hill."

"Who's this young lady with you?" Don squinted at Rayna. "Do I know you?"

"No, sir, I don't think we've met." Rayna held out her hand to Don and the dog, Jax, gave a little growl. She looked at the old dog. "It's OK, Jax. I'm friendly."

"Don't let him fool ya. He is, too." Mr. Hill told her.

Rayna put her hand down to Jax's nose. He sniffed her a little and then licked her hand and wagged his tail. "Good boy." Rayna said.

"Mr. Hill," Wolf motioned toward Rayna, "this is Rayna, the investigator I told you about."

"Weren't you on the TV?" The old man asked.

"Yes, sir. A few years ago, I was."

"I knew you looked familiar. What are you doing here with him?" Don looked puzzled.

"Well, sir, I investigate unusual things that happen around here. Mr. Wolf told me that you had an unusual story, so here I am."

"So you don't do the weather anymore?"

"I do, but not on TV anymore. The investigation is sort of a hobby and volunteer work that I do on the side." Rayna said.

"Oh… I see," Don said.

Wolf interrupted, "Mr. Hill, why don't you tell Rayna what you told me."

"Oh… oh… yes. First, can I get you something? Some tea or lemonade?" The old man asked.

"No, thank you." Rayna and Wolf answered at the same time.

"Oh. OK. Well," Mr. Hill began, "it was last week sometime. I was down the hill over there." He pointed down the drive past a deteriorating garage. "I was pulling weeds out of the garden when I heard this noise, ya see. It was kind of like a hum, and it seemed to be coming from nowhere and everywhere." He paused for a second and nodded his head as if confirming the facts for himself. "I thought it might be from up the mountain above me, but at the same time it sounded like it was coming from the valley or the woods. I couldn't figure it out."

"You said that you've never heard it before?" Wolf asked.

"Nope. I never heard nothin' like it before. I've lived up here nearly fifty years and never heard that sound till that day."

Rayna asked, "Did Jax respond to it?"

"Oh, he did. He most certainly did. He came running up to me and stood on alert, hackles up, ears up, and nose in the air. His eyes were darting everywhere. He couldn't place it either. Then he started howlin'. You got to understand, this dog is quiet. You heard his bark a minute ago. He ain't gonna scare nobody with that. That day he howled like nobody's business. Then it was gone. Just like that… gone."

"Have you heard it since?" Wolf asked.

"No, sir." Don Hill looked at Rayna. "What do you think it was?"

"I'm not exactly sure, sir. Mr. Wolf here heard something similar today, and a family on the other side of Jupiter did, too. It doesn't seem to be confined to this mountain."

"Well, I don't want to ever hear that again. It was unearthly." Don said. "Mr. Wolf, you heard it today?"

Wolf answered, "I can't be sure it was the same hum, but it sounded much like you described it to me."

"Over on your side of the mountain?" Don's face showed concern.

"Over in the park area on Bell Mountain," Wolf answered.

"Hm… I guess I'm glad I ain't the only one who heard it."

"Mr. Hill, do you have any guesses as to what it might have been? Did it sound like anything you've heard in the past? I know you said you've never heard it before, but have you heard anything *like* it?" Rayna asked.

"I've tried, ma'am. I can't think of anything. It wasn't a chopper or a saw or a drill or nothin'. It was just a hum, and it filled the air around here. I couldn't figure out where it was coming from. It just came up, sounded for a few minutes, got Jax upset, and then stopped." The old man patted his mutt on the head.

"Thanks for answering our questions," Rayna said.

"Well, I was hoping for some answers myself." Don said. "I guess you can't give what you don't have."

Rayna nodded her head in agreement. "Unfortunately, that's true. If I find anything out, though, Mr. Wolf or I will let you know."

Wolf agreed, "We'll keep you posted, Mr. Hill."

"Thank ya." He shook Rayna and Wolf's hands. "Y'all have a good night and drive safely, ya hear?"

"Yes, sir!" Wolf answered, and he and Rayna took their leave.

The drive back to Jupiter was only about twenty minutes long. As Wolf drove the jeep back down the mountain into the valley, Rayna was lost in thought. "What could be the cause of the noise? Why is this suddenly happening? Why here in eastern Tennessee? Is it happening in other places?" The questions were racing through her mind.

Wolf's cell phone rang in his shirt pocket. He glanced at Rayna. "Do you mind if I take this?"

"No, not at all."

Looking at the caller ID, he added, "Not sure if I want to." Then he held the phone to his ear. "Hello?"

Rayna politely tried not to eavesdrop, but the phone broke her train of thought. Besides, it was hard not to listen to the only conversation in the vicinity.

Wolf seemed aggravated. "Hi, Jess... You're what?" There was a long pause, and Rayna could hear a female's voice chattering through the phone. "Jess... c'mon... I don't think we agreed on dinner tonight. No... you said last Sunday, 'this is nice.' I said 'yes, it is.' That doesn't constitute an agreement to do it every Sunday. Since when do we do anything like a normal couple?"

"Now this is awkward," Rayna thought to herself.

"Well, put it in the fridge and have it for lunch." The argument continued. "I already ate. I have other things to do tonight... Well, you should have asked... Fine!" Wolf turned off the phone and put it back in his pocket.

Rayna was alternating between staring out the window and in her side view mirror. She thought that it had to be obvious that she was not comfortable with witnessing Wolf's side of the exchange.

"I'm sorry," Wolf said.

"No problem. Girlfriend?"

"No. I mean not really." Wolf stared at the road in front of him. "We go out on occasion. I thought we had an understanding. Nothing gets serious. Then every once in a while, she pulls this crap."

"Crap?" Rayna asked. Then she saw something in the side view mirror that made her hold her breath.

14

At first, she thought it could be the lights on the underside of a helicopter, but as they got closer, Rayna realized they weren't attached to anything. She looked over her shoulder out of the passenger side window and witnessed two glowing orbs. They were between the size of basketballs and beach balls and skimming the tree line as they approached the Jeep. Wolf noticed something else had her attention, so he slowed the Jeep and craned his neck to see what Rayna was seeing.

The orbs seemed to be playing follow the leader as they came to a point in front of the Jeep and then rounded back toward the tree line on Wolf's side. They both started out a bright reddish-orange color. The one in front changed to green, and then the second one did the same. Wolf had to turn his head and look over his shoulder to keep them in view as long as possible. In just moments it was over, but the whole thing felt like it happened in slow motion.

Wolf turned his attention back to driving. He had slowed the Jeep down to a crawl to be able to get a good look without leaving the road. Rayna took a deep breath and let it out slowly. For a minute there was silence as they processed what they had just witnessed.

At the same time, Rayna and Wolf both asked each other, "What was that?" Neither had an answer.

"I didn't hear any sound," Rayna said in disbelief.

"Me, neither."

"It was like they were playing follow the leader," Rayna observed. "I don't know what that was..." her voice trailed off. Wolf said nothing. He didn't know what to say.

Chapter 3

Rayna looked at her watch when Wolf crossed into Jupiter's town limits. "9:00pm, how did it get so late that fast?"

"I guess time flies, huh?" Wolf said.

"That explains why I'm a little hungry again."

"Me, too."

Wolf drove Rayna back to her house where they had left her truck before driving out to see Don Hill. From the outside, Rayna's home looked very simple with white painted siding and a wrap-around porch. A light at the front of the house illuminated a double seated, wooden glider next to the front door. A second light on the driveway side of the house showed the more often used side door. Rayna noticed a light shining through the window to the right of the front door as Wolf pulled into her driveway. It seemed a little odd, but not surprising, given that she knew the light had been turned off when she left, but it never remained that way for long.

"Well, here we are." Rayna announced. "I think I'm going to heat up a frozen pizza, or something. I've got a ton of research to do tonight, so I might as well have a snack. Would you like some?"

Wolf considered the offer for a moment, and then turned off the Jeep's engine. "That sounds great."

The side door entered into the kitchen where Rayna immediately turned on the oven. Wolf noted how new everything looked. The stove had a flat top, the fridge was shiny stainless steel, and the cabinets practically glowed.

"Nice," Wolf said.

"Thanks. I just renovated the kitchen and the bathrooms." Rayna smiled with pride. "This house is over one hundred years old. I think before me the last time anybody renovated it was in the 50's."

"How long have you been here?"

"About a year, but I've owned it for almost two. It had been sitting empty for a long time. The last owners didn't want to live in it and couldn't sell it. They gave up. The bank took it over, and I got it for a steal."

"Really?"

"Pennies on the dollar, but it needed a lot of work. It had been empty for so long that nature was starting to take it over. We had to do some structural work before I could move in."

"We?"

"Well, mostly me. My family helped when they could. I hired a guy to do the hard stuff. Now it's livable, so I'm updating each room as I can afford it."

"I'm impressed," Wolf said.

"Would you like the not-so-grand tour? I mean after seeing the kitchen, the rest of the house is pretty unimpressive."

Wolf nodded, and Rayna led him through a doorway into the living room at the front of the house. The high ceiling was surprising, but the dull, scratched wooden floor was not given the age of the house. An eclectic combination of furniture, framed photos, and antiques filled the room.

"This is my next project," Rayna declared. "The floors need refinishing and I'm going to update the light fixtures. The crown molding was here to begin with."

They walked through another doorway into a hall that ran the depth of the house from the front door to the back door. Directly across the hall from the living room was a larger room.

"At some point, I think this was the living room and the room we were just in was the dining room. Now this is my office and library."

Wolf walked around the room looking at the wall-to-wall bookshelves. "Were these here?" he asked.

"No, I had them built in. I always wanted a library like this with dark wood, a nice big desk and a leather chair or two. I know it's a masculine look, but I love it."

"It's nice," Wolf said. Then he looked a little closer at Rayna's book collection. "Weather, climate, earth sciences..." he walked over to the next wall of books. "... Ghosts, spirits, intuition, ancient mysteries, UFO's, and cryptids?"

Rayna smiled sheepishly. "Surprised?"

"I would have been more surprised this morning, but after meeting you this evening... not so much." He pulled a large book about UFO's off the shelf. "Anything like what we saw in here?"

"I don't think so, but I'm planning on scanning that one and a few others tonight. I'll probably do an internet search, too."

"Not planning on sleeping, huh?"

"Probably not much, no. I know myself well enough to know my brain will probably not shut down easily after today's events. If I can't sleep, I might as well be productive, right?"

"Right," Wolf agreed.

Rayna heard a muffled thud down the hall and stopped to listen. Wolf heard it, too, and paused. They heard another one. Rayna excused herself and followed the sound down the hallway to the next room. Wolf followed. The door was closed. "I never shut this," Rayna said quietly.

Thud.

Rayna opened the door cautiously. Her cat, Cloud, came running out from inside the room, screaming meows. Wolf jumped back, took a deep breath, and laughed. "Phew! Hey, Kitty!" He said.

Cloud stopped halfway to the back door and looked back at them. She meowed again.

"Cloud, sweetie," Rayna said. "Come here." The black cat seemed to calm down immediately at the sound of Rayna's soft tone. She walked to Rayna's feet, sat down, looked up, and gave a quiet meow. Rayna bent down and scooped her up. "What were you doing in there?" Rayna asked. Cloud started purring as Rayna scratched behind her ear.

"You named your black cat 'Cloud'?" Wolf said with a grin and reached over to pet Cloud's head. The cat's green eyes seemed to smile at him.

"She's my little Black Storm Cloud. Although sometimes I think I should have named her 'Fido.' She really has the personality of a guard dog sometimes."

"Except when she shuts herself in a bedroom."

"Um… right." Rayna was pretty sure the cat hadn't closed the door on her own or turned on the lamp in the office.

Before Rayna shut the door to the empty bedroom, she glanced around to see that nothing was out of place. She closed the door and said to Wolf, "Shall we continue?"

Thud.

Wolf heard it, too. He pointed to the bedroom door that Rayna had just closed with a quizzical look on his face. Rayna opened the door again and said "Cut it out, okay?" Once more, she closed the door and looked at Wolf. He was staring at her with one eyebrow cocked.

"Who are you talking to?" he asked.

"I don't know," she answered.

"Really?"

"Yes." Rayna started walking down the hallway toward the second bedroom.

"If I didn't know better, I'd say that the paranormal investigator is hiding a ghost of her own."

"I'm not 'hiding' anything. I'm choosing to ignore him at the moment."

"Him? Does he have a name?"

"I call him 'Grumpy.'" Rayna said with a smile.

"I'm sure he loves that." Wolf and Rayna, still holding a loudly purring Cloud, were standing in her bedroom.

"He gets called Grumpy because he showed up when I started renovating. He scared a few people away early on. Between him and my black cat, my sister won't visit me after dark. The first contractor I hired left without a word one day. When I called him, he told me to hire someone else."

"How do you know that Grumpy is a he?"

"I just know."

"Is he evil?"

"No, he's just grumpy. He's not happy that I'm changing things so he makes noises, hides things, and occasionally shows himself."

Wolf seemed genuinely interested. "He shows himself? As in a full-bodied apparition?"

"Not quite," Rayna answered. "When I see him, I see light... like the shimmer of a silver Mylar balloon. That's the only way I can describe it. Either I'm not strong enough to see more of him, or he's not strong enough to fully materialize."

"That's kind of cool."

"So are you sensitive at all?" Rayna asked.

"A little, maybe." Wolf changed the subject. "Do you sleep in this room?"

Rayna blushed a little when she realized that she had a gorgeous man standing in her bedroom for the first time in a long time. "Yeah."

Wolf looked around. "I'm kind of surprised."

"Why?"

"You've obviously spent time and money on some of your other rooms, but you haven't touched this one yet."

"I'm saving the bedrooms for last. I don't do anything but sleep in here..."

"That's too bad," Wolf said quietly.

"... So, I'm saving it for later." Rayna knew Wolf said something but wasn't sure what. "What did you say? I missed it."

"Nothing," Wolf smiled.

In the kitchen, the stove beeped twice. "Hmm... let's go put that pizza in the oven," Rayna said.

Wolf glanced at Rayna's nightstand on his way out of the room. He saw a small, red suede, hand sewn pouch sitting next to a piece of amethyst, a stack of books and magazines, a notebook, her alarm clock and a small vile of clear liquid with a red cross drawn on it in marker. "Interesting," he thought to himself.

The two made small talk over pizza. Afterwards, Wolf excused himself and drove home. Rayna returned to her library and spent the rest of the night looking for UFO reports describing something similar to what they witnessed. At 4:00am, her computer froze completely, and at 4:30 she finally went to bed.

Chapter 4

The next morning, the sheriff's office was nearly deserted when Rayna arrived. Barb was at the front desk facing the double glass entry doors. Her blonde hair was tied in a loose bun on the back of her head and her reading glasses were sitting low on her nose. Rayna could see that she was chatting away, but she didn't appear to be holding a phone. When she entered, Rayna saw no one. "Who are you talking to?"

"Baby brother," Barb answered and pointed down beside her to the floor behind the reception desk.

Rayna peered over the desk in the direction Barb pointed. On the floor, sitting cross-legged and putting the cover on a computer tower was Lee. He looked up at Rayna with a big grin, his green eyes shining, "Hello, Gorgeous!"

"Just the man I was hoping to see!" Rayna greeted him.

He jumped to his feet. "Really?"

"Yes, sir!"

"You don't know how long I've waited to hear that! So, what will it be? Dinner and a movie? Picnic on the lake?"

"How about 'computer in my truck'?" Rayna smiled, but Lee's grin shrank a little.

"What?" He asked.

"My laptop froze completely this morning. I can't get it to do anything." Rayna answered. "If you can thaw it out or bring it back to life, I'll pay you."

"No payment necessary. Just let me take you out."

"I'll pay you," she reiterated. Lee had been asking her out since high school, and never accepted "no" for an answer, not even after a million nos. He was relentless, but Rayna had gotten accustomed to it. She could tell when he wasn't feeling well by how few times he asked for a date during a conversation.

Lee was a handsome guy with those big, green eyes, short, sandy blonde hair, and a small frame. He had a reputation for spoiling the women he dated. He also had the reputation for dating more than one at a time, which was a turn-off for Rayna. Add his reputation to the fact that he was Barb's brother, and Rayna never had a problem saying "no."

"Did you try control alt delete?" Barb asked.

"Of course, I did," Rayna answered. "I also tried unplugging it and plugging it back in when all else failed. Nothing happened. It's unresponsive."

"Lee cracked his knuckles as if in preparation. "Let me have a go at it."

"Thanks, Lee!" Rayna said. "I'm in trouble without that laptop. My whole life is in there."

"You don't have a back-up drive?" Barb asked.

"I do for the company files, but not for my personal stuff."

"Have you learned nothing from me?" Lee asked.

Rayna answered, "Only that you're relentless when you put your mind to something and an I.T. genius."

Lee smiled. "OK. You learned *about* me, but not *from* me." He looked outside through the double doors toward Rayna's truck. "Let's go have a look."

After Lee agreed to take Rayna's laptop home that afternoon and attempt to fix it, Rayna returned to Barb inside. "Well, Barb, you lucked out."

"What do you mean?"

Rayna answered, "That ranger that sounded cute on the phone – you remember – the one you should not have just given my info to…"

"Yes?" Barb sat straight up behind the desk and gave a sly grin.

"Oh my gosh, girl!" Rayna couldn't hide her excitement. "He was way beyond cute. He was hot!"

"I knew it!"

"But," Rayna warned, "don't do that again. You know I don't like strangers having my number."

"Sorry," Barb pretended to mean it. "So are you going out with him?"

"I don't know about that."

"Why not?"

"He's got someone, I think. It seems to be kind of on again, off again."

"So, it's on?"

"I don't know. They kind of had a tiff on the phone while we were in his Jeep."

"Rayna, go for it! Geez!" Barb hated seeing Rayna alone all the time. "You really need a man in your life."

"I have no time for a man in my life."

"You have to make time."

Rayna turned away from the desk to look outside and decided to change the subject. "Do you want to know what I saw last night?"

"You mean other than a hot guy?"

"He saw it, too." Rayna did her best to describe what she could only term an unidentified flying pair of objects.

"Were you frightened?" Barb asked.

"Not really. It was more like I was intrigued. I'm not sure about Wolf. He was hard to read."

"Are you going to report it?"

"To whom? In the case of UFO's, I'm as much an authority as the sheriff is. Plus, I think he'd rather not hear it."

"Rayna, what if what you saw last night was linked to the horse case?"

"It wouldn't surprise me if it is all linked, but there's no way to know for sure."

"The sheriff would want to know."

"Then you can mention it to him," Rayna said, "and if he wants a full report made, he can ask me for it. I'm not hiding anything. I just don't think he'll be interested. He's told me before that the paranormal is my realm and the explainable is his."

"That's true." Barb took her turn to change the subject. "So when are you going to see him again?"

"Who?"

"Shut up! Who? You know who! The hot ranger, of course!"

Rayna smiled at her friend. "Soon, I guess. After all, we are working a case together."

Chapter 5

The sun had barely risen over the late July horizon before Rayna's phone rang the next morning. She looked at the screen before answering. "Hi, Barb, what's up?"

Barb's voice was shaky and full of fear. "Lee's missing!"

"What?" Rayna sat up in her bed.

"He's missing! We can't find him! He didn't call me last night like he was supposed to. I figured he was on a date. I drove past his house this morning, and his car wasn't there."

"So, he spent the night with his date."

"No! He didn't have a date!"

"Barb…"

"He's not answering his phone. This isn't like him!"

"Don't panic." Rayna tried to keep her own voice soothing. Lee might be a bit of a womanizer, but it wasn't like him to not call his sister to check in. The two had always been close, so close that people thought they were twins. Just 18 months apart, they looked close enough in age to fool most people. Lee was just a year behind her and always beside her outside of classes at school. They didn't have any space between them really until Lee went to the university after high school and Barb stayed home and took a few classes at the community college.

"Dean is keeping his eyes open, but he says it's too early to file a missing persons report."

"I'm sure Lee's fine, Hon. Where was he going after he left us yesterday?"

"Out for lunch and then home to look at your laptop, I guess."

"Did he make it to lunch?"

"I don't know…" Barb's voice trailed off.

23

"There are only three restaurants in this town. Everyone knows him. Call and see if he ate at any of them."

"OK." Now that she had a plan, Barb's voice grew stronger. "OK. I'll call them."

"I'm on my way down to see you, OK?"

"OK."

When Rayna arrived at the Sheriff's Office, Barb's eyes were red and her face was blotchy. She was sitting behind the desk being consoled by a young, round-faced deputy. He was handing her tissues as she tried to wipe the mascara from under her eyes.

"Any news?" Rayna asked.

The deputy shook his head. "I keep telling her it's too soon to be so worked up."

"I know my brother." Barb choked back more sobs. "He doesn't do this."

Rayna knew Lee, too. The three of them grew up together. Barb was the wild one. Lee was girl-crazy, but predictable. Barb was right: disappearing was not like Lee. The sheriff's voice on the deputy's radio interrupted Rayna's thoughts. "Wilkerson?"

The deputy answered, "Yes, sir."

"Are you still with Barbara?" The radio crackled.

Again, Wilkerson answered, "Yes, sir."

"Ask her if her brother still drives a white Mustang."

Barb nodded her head slowly. "Why?" she whispered.

"She says 'yes,' Sheriff." The deputy turned his back to Barb as if to shield her from what came next.

The sheriff's voice stated, "We've got a report of an abandoned white mustang at Bell Mountain Recreation Area. The ranger... um... Wolf... is closer. He's going to check it out. We're on our way up there."

"10-4," the deputy answered.

"I'm going!" Barb jumped up from the desk sending her wheeled chair crashing into the wall behind her.

Wilkerson grabbed her arm. "Wait, Barb!" She shook free from his grasp, and he looked back at Rayna for help.

"I can't stop her." Rayna told him. She stepped in front of Barb as her friend rounded the desk. "You're in no shape to drive." Barb paused. "We'll take my truck."

"Thanks," Barb whispered.

Wilkerson radioed back to the sheriff. "Barb's on her way. Rayna is bringing her."

Rayna was cautious about her speed on the way to Bell Mountain. She wanted to give the sheriff time to get to the scene before she and Barb arrived.

Barb sat in the passenger seat babbling. Her words were alternating between hopeful and hopeless. She seemed totally unaware of the car's velocity.

"It will be okay, Barb," Rayna assured her.

"How do you know?"

"I just know." Rayna looked at her best friend sitting beside her.

"But how?"

"Barb, you know me. I can't tell you how. I just know. Have I ever been wrong?" Barb's face went blank. "When it really mattered?" Rayna added.

"No," her friend conceded and smiled weakly.

"He's alive. I don't know where, but I'm sure he's alive." Rayna realized at that moment that she was driving the stretch of road where she and Wolf had witnessed the balls of light. "What if the lights and Lee's disappearance were connected?" she thought to herself. "Is it just a coincidence..."

Barb interrupted Rayna's train of thought. "Lee always loved you."

"So he's said."

"No, really. He wanted to date you in high school, but you were too busy with guitar boy."

"Guitar boy was my type." Rayna really didn't want to revisit past loves. "Lee always had a girl. He wasn't lonely. He's never been lonely."

"True." Barb settled into her seat and took a deep breath. She was calmer for the moment. "He still loves you."

"And I love him like a brother. You're like my sister, Barb. I couldn't date him."

"I know. It would be weird for all of us."

"Exactly! What if we broke up?"

"Or worse, got married!" Barb laughed.

"Hey now!" Rayna was happy to hear that laugh.

"You really think he's okay?"

"I'm sure he is." In her mind's eye, Rayna got a quick glimpse of an emergency room. At least, that's what she thought it was. There were people who looked sick and battered sitting in rows of chairs against gray walls. She didn't see Lee in her vision, but knew it had to be related. She opted not to mention it to Barb.

Despite the anxious mood in the car, Rayna's heart fluttered a bit when she saw Ranger Wolf waive at her from beside the white Mustang. His long hair was pulled back under the hat that shielded his blue eyes from the sun.

"Oh, God!" Barb gasped. "That's Lee's car!" She reached for the door handle before the truck was in park.

"Hold on!" Rayna said. "Let me stop the truck first!"

In the blink of an eye, Barb was outside the truck and running toward her brother's Mustang. Rayna was behind her as quickly as possible.

The sheriff stepped in front of Barb before she could reach Lee's car. "He's not here, Hon," he said and gently grabbed her arms with both hands.

"Where is he?" Barb was panicked again.

25

"We don't know. There's no sign of him."

Rayna arrived at Barb's side and put an arm around her. The sheriff released his grasp and motioned with a nod of his head for Rayna to guide her friend away from the Mustang.

"Where is he?" Barb asked again.

Rayna led her to a parking space between the sheriff's car and Wolf's Jeep. "We'll find him." Barb started to cry and buried her face in Rayna's shoulder. "It'll be okay," Rayna assured her as she raised her eyes to see Wolf walking toward her.

"Hi," he said. Barb turned around at the sound of his voice, tears streaming down her cheeks.

Rayna grinned slightly. She couldn't help herself. "Hi, Wolf."

"Wolf?" Barb repeated quietly looking back at Rayna.

"This is my friend Barb." Rayna introduced them. "Barb, this is Ranger Steven Wolf."

"Nice to meet you," Wolf said. "I'm sorry it's under such stressful circumstances."

"I'm sure the sheriff explained that Barb is Lee's sister." Rayna said. "That's his car."

"Yes, he did."

"Can you tell us anything?" Barb asked.

"Not much. I got a call about a car that was here when we opened the gates this morning. Overnight parking is prohibited. Then I heard on the scanner that a man in Jupiter might be missing and they described the car. So, I came down here and called the sheriff."

Barb looked defeated. "That's it?"

"Sorry," Wolf answered. "That's all I've got. I mean, it does look a little suspicious."

"How do you mean?" Rayna questioned.

"I mean, the trunk was open and empty. There's no sign of him, no sign of a struggle around the vehicle, and no sign of a second car. Yet, there are no footprints to show that he just parked it and walked away either."

"So the car was empty?" Barb asked.

"Completely?" Rayna added.

"Yes."

"Nothing was in the trunk?" asked Rayna.

"Nothing." Wolf answered. "Why?"

"He had my laptop in there. He was going to fix it."

"Maybe he already dropped it at home," Barb suggested.

"Maybe." Rayna repeated.

After a few hours of standing around while the officers and rangers scoured the parking lot for clues, Barb and Rayna had become equally frustrated. When the sheriff felt that his men had searched enough, he agreed to take Barb back to the office even though she was in no frame of mind to get any work done. Rayna stayed behind waiting for the car to be taken back to town and wondering if it was truly the scene of a crime. The fact that there was no blood and no sign of any struggle seemed like a good indicator that Lee would be alright. Rayna thought back to the little flash of an emergency room that she had on the way to the mountain. If Lee was there, where was it? Surely none of the towns near Jupiter had a hospital with an E.R. of the size she envisioned. Most of these towns were lucky to have a small doctor's office or a decent clinic. The largest clinic, in fact, was in Jupiter since it was the county seat. If Lee were there, the sheriff would have known immediately.

As Rayna thought about it, she realized she was looking at an odd shape in the grass about 40 feet from Lee's car. Out of curiosity, she walked closer. "Oh, Ranger?" she called over her shoulder to Wolf, who was sitting in his Jeep talking on his radio to a coworker about the missing man.

"Wolf paused his conversation. "Yes?"

"What do you make of this?"

"Hang on. I'll be right there." He ended his radio conversation with "I'll update you later." Then, he got out of his vehicle and walked over to Rayna's side. "Huh. I've never seen that before."

Rayna was pointing at a large triangular shape that appeared to be burned into the grass. It was about ten feet across, symmetrical, and had a circle within each of the three points. "Nobody noticed this earlier?"

"I guess we were all too focused on the car and the area directly surrounding it." Wolf looked at Rayna. "What do you make of it?"

"I'm not sure," she answered and started walking the perimeter of it. "It's unusual, right?" I mean, you've never seen it before, right?"

"Never."

"It could be fake."

"Fake what though?" Wolf seemed clueless, and Rayna wasn't sure if he was genuinely baffled, or not.

"Um..." Rayna looked for a way to approach the subject. "Maybe you should read more UFOlogy books."

"What?"

"This is a classic shape reported at alleged UFO landing sites."

Wolf stared at Rayna for a minute. "Come again?"

"I'm not kidding, and I know you heard me." Rayna kneeled down and almost touched the matted down, crispy grass that created the outline. She stopped herself momentarily, remembering stories of physical ailments that occurred in reaction to contact with things such as this odd triangle. One woman lost feeling in her hand after touching the ground at a landing site. Rayna stood up straight. "Do you have any gloves?"

"You're not telling me a UFO landed here." Wolf was still staring.

"No, I'm not. Like I said, it could be faked." Rayna walked back around the perimeter toward Wolf. "Until we know what caused it, I'm not touching it without gloves." She raised both hands to eye level and wiggled her fingers. "Got any?"

"Yeah, they're in the back of my Jeep."

"Wolf retrieved his gloves from the back of his vehicle, and Rayna grabbed her go-bag from hers. It was a khaki cloth tote bag with red stamped impressions of ghosts, crosses and tombstones. Inside it was her still camera, mini-video camera, a K-2 meter, notebook, measuring tape, thermometer, a digital voice recorder, dowsing rods, and extra batteries. She fumbled through it for her camera first.

Wolf looked at the bag and chuckled. "What is that?"

"My go-bag. It has most of what I use on investigations."

"You carry it with you everywhere?" he asked while peering into the bag.

"Do you carry your gun with you everywhere?" She asked, motioning to the handgun in its holster on his belt.

"Actually, no."

The answer took Rayna by surprise. "No? Really?"

"I only wear it when I'm on duty or expecting the unexpected."

"Oh. I've learned to always expect the unexpected." She started taking photos of the triangle. "Years ago, I'd only carry it when I knew I was going on an official investigation. Then something would pop up spur of the moment, and I'd kick myself for not having it with me. Now, it's like a second purse – always with me." She looked at Wolf who had a grin on his face. "What?"

"I can honestly say that I've never met a woman like you before."

Rayna blushed a little. "Is that a good thing, or a bad thing?"

"I'm not sure yet," he answered.

Rayna took the measuring tape out of her bag and handed him the end. "I need help with this part," she said. He understood and walked to the end of the one of the sides of the triangle. Rayna backed up until she was at the other end, and took a reading and a photo of her end of the tape. "Nine feet, seven inches," she read. They repeated this on each of the other two sides, which were perfectly equal. Then, Rayna pulled the K-2 meter out of her bag.

"What's that for?" Wolf asked pointing at it. She held it up for his inspection. It was an odd shaped, hand-held instrument with a switch on the side and LED lights in an arc shape on the top at one end.

"This is a K-2 meter," she answered. "It measures electro-magnetic fields. The green light on the left is normal; the red is high." While she spoke, she crossed into the triangle and the K-2 started blinking from green to yellow to orange. "See?" Rayna walked to the center of the triangle, and the meter spiked to red. She walked back out of the triangle and stood next to Wolf, and it went back to green again. "Hm..." she said, aiming the detector at him. "You're normal." She grinned and handed him the video camera after turning it on. "Do you mind?"

Wolf took the camera. "Sure, what am I doing?"

"Just point and shoot. I want the K-2 documented as I walk around this area." Rayna walked the outside of the perimeter of the unusual triangle first. Then she crisscrossed the inside, narrating as she moved with slow, deliberate steps. She took the camera back from Wolf when she was done. "So, what's your professional opinion, Ranger?"

"This is definitely unusual to say the least. I would never have thought to use a... What is it? K-2 meter?"

"It's second nature when you've been investigating the 'unusual' as long as I have." She opened her notebook and wrote down the measurements she had gathered. "Do you think this has anything to do with Lee?"

"I have no idea," Wolf answered. "It's certainly at least a very strange coincidence."

"You've never had reports of anything like this in the park before?"

He shook his head. "Not to my knowledge."

Chapter 6

The next morning was thick with humidity and distant thunder. Cloud made a sound of disapproval when Rayna ushered her outside and shut the storm door quickly behind her. "You're the one who doesn't like a litter box," Rayna said through the glass as she watched her little black cat stand facing the yard flicking her tail in protest. Cloud looked back at Rayna with pleading eyes. "No, ma'am. Now go do your business."

Rayna could have stood there longer and continued the argument, but she heard her phone ringing in the kitchen. Her cell phone had a special ring for calls coming from the sheriff's office. She hurried to pick it up before the call was sent to voicemail. "Hello?"

"Is this Rayna Smith?" She didn't recognize the young man's voice on the other end.

"Yes, it is. Can I help you?"

"Miss Smith, this is Deputy Thomas. Barbara asked me to call you on her behalf. Her brother has been found."

"Found? Where?"

"Well, more like he turned up at St. Regis Hospital in Knoxville. She's on her way there with the sheriff. She left her cell phone on the desk here and called back by radio asking me to let you know."

"Do you know if he's okay?"

"I think so, but the details are sketchy. They're going to pick him up now, so my guess is that he is well enough to be coming back home to Jupiter."

"Okay. Thank you, Deputy, for letting me know."

"Yes, ma'am," he said and immediately hung up.

Rayna stood with her phone in her hand staring blankly into space. So, Lee was alive and apparently alright, but how did he end up in a private hospital in Knoxville? What happened between the time he left with her computer and now? When and where did he get separated from his car? And where was her laptop?

A tap on the storm door interrupted the barrage of questions in her mind. She half-expected to see Cloud's head peaking through the lower part of the glass, but instead she saw Sam standing there on her porch with his usual smile. "Hey, Sam!" she greeted him as she opened the door. A blur of black fur shot past her leg before Sam could even return her greeting.

"Hi, Rayna. Cloud wanted in."

"No kidding," Rayna smirked and stepped aside so that Sam could enter. "I just got a call. Lee's been found."

"That's what I was coming over to tell you. I heard it on the scanner." Rayna occasionally forgot that, first and foremost, Sam was a newsman. The police scanner was always running in his office and often in his home.

"Why didn't you just call me?"

Sam smiled. "Because I knew you'd have food here. I've been too busy to do my grocery shopping. Have you had breakfast yet?"

"Not yet," she answered leading him into the kitchen where he promptly opened the refrigerator.

"Hmm… I think I can make this work." He pulled out a carton of eggs, milk, and butter.

"I'll start the coffee," Rayna said.

While the old friends made a breakfast of scrambled eggs, bacon and toast, they discussed all of the possible reasons they could think of behind the recent events. UFOs, government conspiracies, and odd coincidences seemed to be the theme lately.

"You know," Sam said between bites, "I read online somewhere that there is a computer virus that attacks when you go to certain UFO-related websites. They say it's part of a government cover-up."

"Or it's just some nut job causing problems for those sites and their readers."

"I know. I know. You've never been big on conspiracy theories."

Rayna took a sip of her coffee. "They're entertaining ideas, but so many of them require more thought to buy into than they are worth. If the easiest explanation is usually the right one, then why are those so convoluted that entire books are written to explain them?"

"Paranoia sells almost as well as sex does." Sam smiled broadly.

"True," Rayna conceded, "but selling books isn't the same as proving theories. None of them have convinced me of anything. Heck! I've read conspiracy theories written about the government seeding the clouds to cause climate change to keep the green-happy liberals in power. How did cloud seeding become politicized?"

"How did the climate become politicized?"

"Like you said, 'paranoia sells'." Rayna picked up their empty plates and took them to the sink. "I just want to know what we're really dealing with here."

"As do I." Sam refilled their coffee mugs. "What does your Ranger Wolf think?"

"My ranger? No," she paused, "Wolf doesn't seem to know what to think, or if he does, he hasn't told me. What we witnessed the night we met fits the definition of a UFO. It was, or they were, unexplained and flying. He is either in some sort of denial about it, or he knows something and he's not letting on."

"Which do you think it is?"

"My guess is denial. He knows that kind of mystery bothers me. I think he'd tell me, or at least hint to me, if he knew."

"You've only known him a few days and he already knows what bothers you?"

"We talked a lot that first night. He was here pretty late before he left and I started researching, trying to find out what we had seen."

"Late, huh?" Sam was grinning over his coffee.

"What is it with you? You and Barb! Stop trying to be my Cupids. I don't need a boyfriend."

"Yes, you do."

"I disagree." Rayna shrugged. "Even if I do, he's not the one for me."

"Why do you say that?"

"He kind of has a girlfriend."

"No ring on his finger means he's free."

"Oh, really?" Sam knew not to make that argument with her. "Really? I seem to recall you being married for a while and never wearing your ring. What about that guy who texted me every day for a month, and didn't wear a ring? Then when I think he might be date-worthy, I find out that he's married with kids! I swear! I can't trust men to do the right thing and wear an outward sign of their marital commitment. Sometimes I wonder why I trust men at all."

"That hurts." He feigned a frown.

"Oh, shut up. You know I trust you." Sam smiled at Rayna. "I freakin' trust you with my life. It's the strangers I have issues with."

Sam put his mug down and put one big arm around her shoulder. "I'm sorry I brought it up. Let's change the subject, shall we?"

"Please." Rayna rested her head on his shoulder for a moment. He was just tall enough to make it comfortable.

"When are we headed back over to the Lovell farm?"

"Wolf and Fieldman are free this afternoon. I was going to call this morning and see if you could come, too," she answered.

"Well, then, let me get my butt back home and do some writing so that I will be free. What time should I meet you there?"

"About one o'clock, I think. I'll confirm with everyone and text you."

Sam kissed her on the forehead. "Then I'll look forward to your text." He grabbed his coat off the kitchen chair and headed for her front door.

"Hey, Sam!" Rayna called from the kitchen. "Take Cloud out with you. She still needs to get some fresh air."

"Will do!" He scooped up the little black fur ball and went out the door.

Chapter 7

The second trip to the horse farm was a little more pleasant. Sure, the case would still be the topic of conversation, but Sylvia Lovell had promised Rayna a tour of the farm and the land surrounding it. The investigators had gone over the area where the horse had been found with a fine-tooth comb. This time, Professor Derek Vincent would be joining them for the purpose of taking soil samples. His goal was to look for anomalies that might give some clue as to how the horse ended up there.

The weather had been mostly dry there since the incident, so the conditions seemed favorable for collecting samples. There was a little breeze out of the south and the wind ruffled the leaves in the trees and blew Rayna's hair into her mouth. She was beginning to regret applying that new, sticky lip gloss. "So, what's the best way to see the farm?" She asked, pulling her hair off her lower lip again.

Sylvia had her hair in a messy ponytail. Her clothes were spotted with brown dirt, and she was standing with gardening gloves in one hand, and the other hand on her hip. "Well, we could pile in the pickup and stick to the dirt road, which is kind of limiting, or we could take the horses."

"Horses?" Sam asked.

"I choose horses." Rayna said at the same time.

Sylvia replied, "I thought you might."

"Not me." Sam said.

"Why not, big guy?" Rayna smirked. She already knew the answer.

"I'll stay here with the professor." Sam looked at Derek, who just nodded. "Yep. We'll be fine right here."

"Ever been on a horse, Sam?" Sylvia asked.

"No, and I don't intend to."

"Why not?"

Sam hesitated, but finally answered, "If you must know, I don't trust any animal that's larger than I am."

"Really?" Sylvia had a look of disbelief.

"Really."

Rayna offered, "We can take the truck if you want to go."

"No. No, I know you've been itching to ride. Go. Enjoy it!"

"Who else is coming?" Sylvia asked.

Fieldman raised his hand.

"Count me in!" Wolf answered.

So the four of them left Sam and the professor to the work of gathering soil samples around the area where the horse was found and in other parts of the farm so they had samples for comparison.

Sylvia's daughter had three horses saddled and ready. She was bringing the fourth horse out of her stall when the group walked into the barn. Shana looked at her mother. "Just four, right?"

"Yes, unless you want to come along."

"No, thanks. I'm going over to Cindy's for a while."

"Oh, you are?"

"May I?" She changed her tone to that of an innocent teenager.

"Yes, but be back by dinner time," her mother told her.

"Cool!" Shana was already a pro at prepping the horses for a ride. It took her only a few minutes to finish. She guided the last horse over to Wolf and grinned. "Um," she started. "This is Zoe. She's really sweet."

"Hi, Zoe," Wolf said and patted the golden brown horse on her nose.

"Ever ride before?" Shana asked.

"Yes, a friend of my parents had a horse farm. We used to visit him a few times a year. It's been a while though."

Sylvia looked at Fieldman. "How about you?"

"I've ridden a few times – trail rides with my daughter when she was younger."

Next, Sylvia asked Rayna the same question. "My grandparents had horses when I was a child. Since then, just a few trail rides. I love them, though." Rayna smiled broadly.

"Miss Rayna," Shana said, "you can have Winny today. She's real easy to handle. It barely takes a heel to get her going. Mr. Fieldman, we'll give you Jack. You've gotta be patient with him. He's never in a hurry, but he'll get you where you want to go."

Rayna walked up to Winny, a smaller, painted brown and white horse, and patted her on the side of the neck. Winny turned her head toward Rayna and nodded her approval.

Sylvia led the trio across the property, which turned out to be much bigger than it looked. There were three barns, a garage, and another storage building that was almost as large as the smallest barn. In addition to the family's house, there was a one room cabin in the woods near a creek that marked the back edge of the property. Sylvia explained that the creek fed into the Santos River. Water rights and usage had always been hotly contested points. The cabin had no plumbing because of watershed rules, but the family used it on occasion when they had visitors, or when Shana wanted to have a sleepover. As they passed, Rayna noticed a stone-built fire pit near the cabin. It looked like it had been used recently. "Mm… s'mores," she thought out loud. Wolf was riding beside her and smiled at her.

"What did you say?" Fieldman asked. His horse was about 20 feet behind them.

"S'mores!" Rayna called over her shoulder. "Keep up, old man!"

"Are you talking to me, or the horse?"

Rayna laughed. "I'll let you decide!" Fieldman was about fifteen years her senior and liked to tease Rayna about her youth. She had no problem returning the favor when the opportunity arose.

"Laugh now, but I'm guessing you'll be equally as sore as I will be tomorrow," Fieldman said.

At the end of the ride, Wolf quickly hopped off Zoe and stood beside Winny. He looked up at Rayna, "Need any help dismounting?"

Rayna smiled. "Thanks, but I think I've got it." Wolf stepped back, and watched her hesitate a moment. Then she shifted her weight and swung her right leg over the horse and down to the ground in one less-than-graceful move. She realized that her tennis shoe was stuck in the stirrup and bounced on her right leg. Wolf stepped up and grabbed her waist, steadying her while she took a moment to free herself. She giggled quietly. "I've never been good at sticking the dismount."

Back at the house, they found Sam and Derek sitting on the front porch sipping iced tea and chatting with Mr. Lovell. "Nice day for a ride, eh?" The professor called to them.

"Beautiful!" Rayna answered. Their host stood and poured four more glasses of tea, emptying the pitcher. "Is that for me?" Rayna asked, graciously taking a glass from his hand. "Thank you!"

"You're welcome. The professor here was just explaining to me what he's hoping to find in those soil samples he collected. I'm not sure I'd be too happy if he found it." Tim Lovell grimaced.

"What we're really hoping to find above all else," Sam said, "is answers. Maybe some answers will help you sleep better at night."

"A loaded gun close by helps me sleep better these days." Tim chuckled.

"Oh, hush!" Sylvia reprimanded him. "You're not sleeping. You're up at every little sound. Gun, or no gun, you're not resting easy."

"But what if they find radiation, or poisoning, or…" he didn't finish the thought.

"Then we cross that bridge when we come to it." Sylvia picked up the empty tea pitcher.

"We can't afford anymore sick horses."

"Have you had a lot of sick horses lately?" Wolf asked.

"We've had a few," Tim answered.

"How recently?" Wolf wondered.

"Last month, three of them took ill within a week. The vet couldn't figure it out, but he had no problem charging us for the visits!"

"Did they get better?" Rayna asked.

"Two did," he answered. "One just lay down and died."

"That one was pretty old," Sylvia said. "It might've just been her time. We thought maybe it was something that got into the feed, but we feed all of them the same. Only three got sick. Plus, they all stayed in different fields. It just didn't make sense. Then you add the one that y'all are investigating..."

"It seems a little odd," Fieldman finished for her.

Rayna looked at Sylvia and Tim and felt their frustration and fears. "Don't worry. We'll do our best to find some answers, whatever they may be."

Sylvia held out her free hand to shake Rayna's. "We appreciate any help you can give us."

"The Sheriff really didn't have much for us. He just came out, looked around, took a report, and said he'd be in touch," Tim explained.

"I know the Sheriff," Rayna said, "and he's got a lot on his hands, but he is definitely looking for answers, too. He was okay with us coming in to help because the circumstances were just a little beyond unusual."

Sam added, "He also knows that he can trust us to keep him up to speed and keep the case as confidential as possible."

"But aren't you a reporter?" Tim asked.

"Yes, but I'm also a gate-keeper," Sam said with a sly grin. "If I want to keep it on the down-low, I can make it take a real long time for the story to go to press, or at least as long as it takes my editor to get wind of it from other sources. Then, when it is time to take the story public, if I'm the writer, I control what facts get out."

"I guess it's good to have a reporter on our side," Sylvia said.

"I'm just doing what I know I'd want someone else to do for me if I were in your position. My professors back in journalism school would fail me for that, but I have to be me, ya know."

"And we love you for who you are," Rayna told him.

Chapter 8

It had been a few days since the group's trip to the horse farm, and Rayna had temporarily put the case out of her mind and focused on her business as she knew she should. Things were going pretty well that morning. The weather was quiet across most of the country with the exception of her own backyard. There it was a bit more unsettled. Rayna was watching a line of storms that had somehow survived the cool overnight hours and crossed western Tennessee. It was now 8:00am, and she had been up since 5:00 that morning trying to decide just how much of a threat the front would be to her clients nearby and in the Mid-Atlantic states. She knew she was going to have to start making some phone calls and writing risk reports soon.

Rayna had just started to organize her thoughts into a succinct report when her cell phone rang. The caller ID said "Prof Vincent," and she decided to answer, "Good morning, Professor!"

"Good morning, Rayna. I hope I didn't wake you." His voice had the deeper tones of a practiced talk show host.

"Wake me? No, sir! I've been up since five staring at my radar and forecast soundings," Rayna assured him.

"I see," he replied. After a brief pause, he continued. "So, I found something interesting about the soil near the creek on the farm."

"What is it?"

"Slightly elevated levels of radioactivity associated with H_3, also known as tritium."

"Really? Do you think that's significant?" Rayna knew a little about tritium, but not enough to feel confident about her understanding of it.

"To be honest," Derek Vincent answered, "I'm not sure. Typically, I wouldn't be too concerned because it breaks down so quickly, but given the circumstances – the farm, the horses, the vicinity of a nuclear power plant, et cetera, this might be worth investigating further."

"That's interesting. There was a hypothesis during the flap of UFO sightings and cattle mutilations of the early '90's in and around the San Luis Valley out west that it was actually government scientists looking for evidence of radiation poisoning killing animals. The UFO's were thought to be simply misdirection.

"It would take a large amount, larger than I found, of tritium over a decent period of time to poison a horse.

"But, it's possible?" Rayna asked.

"I think so." The professor answered. "If you could come by my office, I can give you a copy of the report and go over a few more things with you."

"Will you be there all day?"

"Not, all day. I have to teach a class at 2:00, but I'll be here until then."

"I'll wrap things up here and then come see you. What's your office address?"

The professor gave Rayna his exact location, and she promised to be there before lunch time. She hung up the phone and made quick work of her reports for her clients. The storms were still coming and would gain strength with the daytime heating. Everyone east of the line would have to be alert that day. Then, she called her only employee and asked her to take over the reins a little early that day.

Three crows pretended to be eagles soaring on the air currents. Occasionally, a wave of turbulence would knock them down. With a panicked flap of their wings, they would rise again and return to their dreams. "It must be fun," Rayna thought with a grin, "to pretend to be someone completely different once in a while."

The low deck of stratocumulus clouds continued to move quickly past. Like a long freight train at a lonely crossing, the end was nowhere in sight. The wind whipped the trees around, and the rain would, from time to time, spit down from a passing cloud. To say the weather was unsettled would be kind. A tornado watch had been extended through the late afternoon for the region. Rayna knew she should be at work. "Kate ought to be able to handle it. She'll call if she needs me," she thought.

The case was taking more time away from the company than Rayna would have liked. Kate didn't mind the extra hours since she was saving for her wedding and honeymoon. She'd actually been begging Rayna for more hours. Still, Rayna didn't always feel like Kate had the best work ethic. There was no proof, but there seemed to be something off about their interactions lately. Rayna made a mental note to touch base with a few of her clients and make sure they were happy, which was all that would matter, for the time being anyway.

Rayna realized she was just sitting in her truck staring through the windshield at those silly birds. Time was slipping away. She put the truck in drive and headed toward Eastern Mountain College three towns to her west.

It was 11:00am when Rayna arrived at the professor's office. There really wasn't much to it: four walls, one doorway, a window above each of two desks with a divider between them. Looking around, she saw two filing cabinets with books and manila folders stacked haphazardly on top, and an aged bookshelf full of ancient texts. At least, they looked ancient by the amount of dust on them.

Derek Vincent was sitting at his desk, which was directly across from the doorway reading what looked like a spreadsheet. He looked up when he heard Rayna tap lightly on the door casing. "Good morning, Rayna! How are you?" he greeted her warmly.

"I'm fine. How are you?" Rayna entered and sat down in the little wooden chair in front of his desk.

"I'm well. I take it you found my office pretty easily."

"The office was easy to find. The parking was a bit harder."

"I'm sorry. I forgot to warn you about that."

"No worries," Rayna smiled, "I found a nice visitor's spot a block away."

"Good. Good." He turned the paper he had been studying so that Rayna could see it, too. "These are the preliminary results from two of the soil samples from the scene," he told her.

A gruff "ahem" sounded from behind her, and Rayna turned her attention to the man in the doorway. He walked in stiffly and shuffled through some papers on the other desk in the office. "Don't mind me," he said. He was of medium height with sandy blonde hair, cropped close to his head, rimless glasses, and half of a sunburn. Literally - the left side of his face was burned, but the right side wasn't.

Derek said to Rayna, "Ms. Rayna Smith, I'd like to introduce you to Professor Gregory Hampton."

Rayna held out her hand. "Pleased to meet you," she said with a smile.

Hampton gave her a cold handshake. "The pleasure's all mine." Rayna immediately felt the urge to wipe his energy off her hand by rubbing it on her pants but fought it. "Rayna Smith, huh?" the man asked. "Weren't you a weather girl on TV?" He flashed a smug grin.

"I was. I'm still a meteorologist, just not on TV anymore. I own a private forecasting company."

Hampton seemed to find what he was searching for on his desk and picked up a yellow notebook. "What brings you to our neck of the woods? Are you here to brush up on some real science?"

Rayna bristled the way Cloud would just before hissing, and Derek recognized her growing aggravation. "Rayna," Vincent interceded, "is just here to see me for a minute. I have a report she'd like to read."

"Oh." Hampton deflated a little.

"Yes, I read molecular chemistry reports with my morning coffee right before I dust off the crystal ball to conjure up a forecast." Rayna said with a flare of false ego.

Hampton ignored her sarcasm, stuffed his notebook under his arm, and grabbed an umbrella leaning against the wall near the door. "I'm off to a meeting. Vincent, please lock up if you leave before I return." With that request, he left them alone in the office again.

"No problem," Derek called behind him. Rayna relaxed in the little chair again. "I'm sorry about that," he told her. "He's a bit of a jerk, but I have no control over whom I share this office with. At least, this guy talks. The last guy was so quiet, you would have thought he was mute, but he had no problem speaking in a lecture hall to fifty students."

"No worries," Rayna reassured him. "He's not the first guy to crack on meteorology. Mets have to be tough. We get the education of a rocket scientist and the pay and respect of a 7/11 employee."

"Frustrating?"

"Sometimes. It's fun to play stupid, though, when the same people who call you a clown one day come running for answers about snow in the forecast the next."

"He looks like a clown," the professor said. "He told me he fell asleep on his side at the pool this weekend. I would tease him, but as you can see, he's already crabby enough."

The professor chuckled and turned his attention back to the subject of her visit. "Here's the printout of the soil samples report. I can email it to you as well." He handed her a plastic folder with several spreadsheets inside.

"Thank you."

"You'll see near the creek, here, is where the tritium levels were slightly elevated." He opened the folder in her hands and flipped a few pages, pointing to each as he spoke. "The samples from the pastures seemed normal. The area around the site where the dead horse was found was also normal."

"I guess that's to be expected since the poor thing seemed to have fallen from the sky."

"I also went up to the Bell Mountain parking lot where you suggested."

"And?" Rayna asked.

"I found that in the triangular shaped area, the tritium levels were normal, but there were abnormally high levels of another radioactive substance."

"Really? What?"

"Inconclusive." The professor cocked an eyebrow at her to emphasize the surprise of the discovery.

"Inconclusive? As in you don't know what exactly the substance is? How far down?" Rayna questioned.

"It seemed to have similar properties to radium, and it was just at the surface."

"What area?"

Derek drew a triangle in the air with his hands. "Just inside the triangle. The samples from the area just five feet away on all sides came back normal."

"How elevated are we talking here?"

"Enough to be a little concerned. You didn't touch the ground there, did you?"

"No," she answered, "I had a feeling it was a bad idea."

"Do you know if anyone else did?"

"I don't think so, but that was several days ago. Someone might have since then."

"I hope not. It is enough to cause mild sickness like vomiting, but not enough to kill. Keep an ear out about that. You might want to alert the rangers, too."

Rayna's face mirrored his concern. "Will do. Just to keep it simple, though, I'll call it radium. Thanks for the printout. I've been having too many issues with digital things lately."

"No problem. I'm happy to provide reading material to go with your morning coffee," he said with a smile.

Chapter 9

After leaving the campus of Eastern Mountain College, Rayna headed east and stopped for lunch with her sister in the next little town. Dawn Smith was thirty-eight years old, two years older than Rayna, and about four inches shorter. Rayna liked to joke that Dawn was her little sister even though she was clearly older. The bigger joke really was that Dawn Smith married Reese Smith, which made her Dawn Smith squared, or that's how Rayna liked to tell it. Nerd humor was lost on Dawn, especially bad nerd humor. She was too busy with the life of a housewife and stay at home mom with three small children under the age of five.

The sisters couldn't be more different. Dawn was independent enough in her younger years, but decided she needed a husband and family in order to feel satisfied with her life. Rayna, on the other hand, was content filling the holes in her personal life with work and paranormal investigations. She had decided after a few poor choices in men that she didn't need one to be happy, and she lived that philosophy daily. If she needed a dose of testosterone in her day, she would just drop by the Sheriff's office or call Sam or Fieldman. There were plenty of men around town who'd be happy to spend a little time with her, but none had been interesting enough to her to spend more than just a little time with. Besides, Rayna would rather be single than annoyed. At least, that's what she told herself every time she talked with her sister.

Rayna walked into the buffet-style restaurant and scanned the room for her sister. In the back corner, a cluster of younger people gathered around a tall, clean-cut man caught her eye. Focusing on him, she realized it was Professor Vincent's office-mate, Gregory Hampton, and he looked as though he was pointing at a map on the table. She couldn't make out details, but assumed it was a map based on the size and fold patterns with its edges sticking up in the air as

43

if it didn't want to sit flat on the table. Hampton was very animated but speaking quietly enough that she couldn't hear a word he said. He didn't notice her, and that was fine with Rayna. His energy still gave her a bad feeling, especially after her encounter with him at the school. She wanted to believe it was only because he was a jerk to her, but she knew she didn't like him the minute she was introduced to him.

Rayna found Dawn sitting in a booth near the front window and took a seat across the table from her. "Good morning, or noon, or whatever it is!" She said, looking at her watch.

"Good afternoon!" Dawn corrected her. "So, how's the weather business?"

Rayna smiled. "Always changing."

"No kidding!" Her sister was used to short answers like that from Rayna.

"No, it's good. I've got some new clients in the works, a good forecaster working for me, and the website is pretty popular, gaining users every day." Rayna knew not to go into too much detail with Dawn. She just wasn't that interested in the life of an entrepreneur.

"Is that the same employee you hired last summer?" Dawn asked.

"Yes, Kate. She's pretty good and she wants at least forty hours a week, so it frees me up to do other things."

"Like what?"

"Line up new business, research, and other stuff."

Dawn smirked. "You're talking about the paranormal stuff, aren't you?"

"Mostly."

"Do you ever really find anything?" Her tone was almost patronizing.

"Yes, we get E.V.P., sometimes anomalous photos and usually first-hand experiences. "

"Isn't that what everybody says they get?"

"Of course! It's the easiest stuff to get. A full-body apparition on video is the Holy Grail, but that's because it's nearly impossible to get." Rayna felt like a broken record. Not only did the curious strangers ask these questions, but her family members did, too, repeatedly.

"Have you gotten anything on video?"

"We've gotten a few things, mostly shadows that we can't explain. Once we got a dark mass that sort of blocked out the light source, which told us that *something* was there. Occasionally, the cameras will behave strangely as if someone is messing, physically, with them when we know nobody is in the room."

Dawn shook her head. "That's all too creepy for me!"

"Not enough for us," Rayna replied.

"Well, you can have it!"

"Um... thank you?" Rayna laughed and changed the subject. "I'm starving."

"This place has a pretty good selection. It's Reese's favorite." Dawn pointed to the rows of food bars covered with sneeze guards. Buffets were not Rayna's usual choice for eating out. She'd worked in restaurants to pay her way through school and seen too many people with gross habits go through those lines.

Movement in Hampton's corner of the room took her attention away from the food. The group was getting up and gathering their things to leave. Rayna watched as they left the restaurant, and then one by one got into a car and drove toward Bell Mountain, the opposite direction of the college and Rayna's route home. Hampton never seemed to notice her presence.

"Somebody you know?" Dawn asked. She had been watching Rayna watch Hampton leave.

"Somebody I just met and would rather not know." Rayna answered, and got up to get her food.

The sisters chatted about the kids and all things domestic over lunch. Their visits were always nice despite their differences. When the plates were cleared and the conversation waned, Rayna stood to leave. "What's next for you today?"

Dawn answered, "I'm gonna try to get some laundry done before picking the kids up from daycare when they'll add more to the pile."

"Good luck with that!" Rayna faked a military salute.

"Yeah, right! What about you?"

"I have to meet up with a ranger to discuss UFO's and radiation."

Dawn never totally took Rayna seriously. "Have fun with that!" she laughed.

Rayna left the restaurant and drove toward Bell Mountain. Along the way, she pondered just how different she and her sister had become. Maybe they had always been that way and adulthood had just made their differences more obvious. Some days it seemed amazing they were even related. No matter what, though, they loved each other.

Chapter 10

"What do you know about radium?" Rayna asked the ranger. He was leaning against his Jeep in the parking lot where Lee's car had been found a few days earlier. His hat was pulled down over his brow to shield his blue eyes from the afternoon sun. Rayna was glad he wasn't wearing shades. She enjoyed looking into those eyes, but she was starting to notice that standing close to him made her feel a little out of breath. It was a new feeling for her as far as a guy was concerned. The last time she'd felt that flash of breathlessness, she'd just run a quarter mile trying to catch a neighbor's runaway dog.

"I know that it was discovered by Madame Curie and it can be dangerous." The look on Wolf's face was all business, but his body language was very relaxed with both hands in his pockets and his back against his SUV.

"Is that it?"

He gave a half-laugh. "There's more?"

"Yes, but you actually know enough to get this conversation started."

"Why? Oh, wait! You went to see the professor this morning, right?"

"Yes," she answered. "He had the results back from all of the soil samples, even the ones from here on Bell Mountain."

"And?"

"They were interesting. The samples from the creek bed at the Lovell farm had slightly elevated levels of tritium, which caught our attention. The rest of the samples from there seemed normal. The ones from here are of concern." Her countenance was more serious than Wolf had seen it.

"Radium?" He guessed.

"Yes, but only in a very specific location."

"Where?"

"Inside the triangular area that you and I found when Lee disappeared. *Only* inside," she emphasized. "The samples from outside of it were normal."

"Really?" Wolf looked over Rayna's shoulder toward the ground beyond the lot where they found the odd shape in the grass. "How did you know not to touch the ground there?"

"I'd read stories about radiation contamination at alleged landing sites, and I didn't want to take any chances."

"So this report didn't surprise you?"

"It did a little. I mean, when you read reports like that, you wonder how much of the stories are trumped up. You have to have a little dose of healthy skepticism in order to be a scientist and an investigator."

"How much radium?" Wolf was looking into Rayna's eyes again, and she suddenly felt very warm. It was all she could do not to fan herself.

She took a deep breath and let it out slowly. "Enough to warrant concern. The professor, Derek, said to keep an ear out for reports of symptoms caused by radiation sickness from people after visiting the park like headaches, nausea, skin burns after touching the ground there. It's such a small area, but it's not isolated. It's right there next to where families park."

"So we should block it off?"

"You might want to, or at least get a second opinion and make an official decision. Derek wasn't exactly working for the Park Service. It's up to you how to handle that part."

Wolf stood up straight and looked at the space across the parking lot again, thoughtfully. "I'd rather be safe than sorry. I know it's possible people have already been exposed, but I'd like to prevent any more potential until we know differently." He opened the door to his vehicle and grabbed his radio. "I'll get one of the guys up here with a soil sample kit and we'll send it off this afternoon. In the meantime, we'll put of some caution tape. The only thing is it might cause a bit more of a stir when curious patrons start looking at that spot and realize there's something odd there. If they hadn't noticed it before, they'll definitely notice it now."

"So, what will you tell them if they ask?"

"That we cannot discuss an ongoing investigation," he answered in a well-practiced, official voice.

"Nice!" Rayna smiled and just stood there for a minute trying to catch her breath again. She wondered if he noticed she was having trouble talking loud enough to hear. He seemed oblivious. "I really need to get back to work," she stated.

"Oh?"

"Yeah. My employee is scheduled to leave in an hour and I need to have a chat with her first."

Wolf took a step a little closer to her and she felt her face get hot. She was sure it must be bright red, but he didn't seem to notice. "Thanks for delivering this information in person." There was that warm smile again.

Rayna couldn't fight the urge to take a step back. Having Wolf in her personal space was too much too handle at that moment. She had never had a man make her feel like she wanted to jump into the Arctic Ocean before, but that was the thought that flashed through her mind. "You're welcome," she said quietly. Then, as quickly as she could she trotted to her truck and left for home. In her rear-view mirror she could see Wolf talking on the radio, watching her leave, as she turned out of the South Lot and headed back down the mountain toward Jupiter.

Chapter 11

Kate was sitting in Rayna's library typing away at the computer on Rayna's mahogany desk. She was still young, and she looked like a college student working on a thesis with her hair pulled back in a high, tight, blonde ponytail and her thick framed glasses resting on her nose, she definitely had a studious air about her. Rayna knew Kate was smart when she hired her. Her professors had written glowing letters of recommendation and her grades reflected everything they had said about her. Still, Rayna always felt there was something suspect about her. She wasn't a bad employee, and Rayna trusted her enough to give her a key to her house in order to use her computer and resources for the job. There was just a nagging feeling about her personality that Rayna didn't like.

"Hi, Kate!" Rayna had slipped in quietly through the kitchen door. Kate seemed surprised by her presence.

"Oh, hi, Rayna!" Kate clicked a window on the screen shut and started gathering her belongings to leave. "I was just going."

"So, everything went well?"

"Yeah. The front passed here without much ado. It blew up a bit over near Murphy, but the drier air on the other side of the mountains took the oomph out of it for now. I'm sure with the daytime heating, it will get going again in a few hours." Kate threw her purse over her shoulder.

"So, everyone's been briefed that needs to be?"

"Yes, ma'am!" She smiled, but it wasn't very genuine. That was it! That was what Rayna had a problem with. Kate's smile never seemed real. She always looked like she was hiding a secret.

"Okay, then. Thanks for coming in today on short notice! I'll see you on Friday, right?"

"Yep! Have a good one!" Kate bounced out of the room and out the front door. She bounced like she was a carefree kid, but her face, her insincere look, gave her away. She was up to something.

Before Rayna could ponder what, her phone rang. The caller ID told her it was Barb, and a wave of guilt washed over her. She had been meaning to call and check on Lee. Rumor had it that he had been nauseous and sunburned when the Sheriff and Barb picked him up at the hospital Knoxville. She drew in a breath and answered, "Hi, Barb!".

"Hey, there!" Her voice was upbeat and relaxed. "How's life?"

"I was going to ask you the same thing. I'm so sorry I haven't checked in on you and Lee. Things just keep happening!"

"No worries! I know you've been busy. I ran into Sam, and he filled me in, at least on what he knew. He said he hadn't talked to you yet, today."

"Yeah, I've been running all morning. I still need to call him, too! There's just not enough time in some days." Rayna sank into one of her pub chairs in the library and felt the soft leather give a little under her weight. It was nice to take it easy for a moment. "I started out with work, and then Professor Vincent called, so I ran over to the college. He had something interesting that I needed to tell Wolf about, so I ran over to Bell Mountain. I stopped and had lunch with Dawn on the way."

"How's she doing?"

"She's fine... the same as always."

"How's Wolf doing?"

"He's fine, too. I just gave him some news that he probably didn't want to hear." Rayna stopped mid-thought. "Hey, how's Lee doing? I heard he was suffering from something like a sunburn and nausea. Is that right? Is he better now?"

"He's getting there. He's kind of a mess. He doesn't remember anything. Nothing! Can you believe it? He was nauseous, and his skin looked sunburned, but it's not like a normal sunburn. It's weird. The doctor said it looked like some type of radiation poisoning. They did some tests and think he'll recover fine, but I'm more worried about his mental health. He's not the same. He's not happy-go-lucky-Lee."

"Does he remember being on Bell Mountain?" Rayna was half-hopeful and half-scared of what that answer might be.

"No. He doesn't remember anything beyond coming home from his date that night. Actually, he remembered starting the drive home, but not getting here. It's so weird!"

"Yes, yes, it is." Rayna shook her head. "Are you at work, or at home?"

"I'm at work for the moment. I came in for a half-day. I don't like leaving him alone too long like this."

"I don't blame you. I need to call Sam, but I'll come visit you later. I promise!"

"Okay. I'll talk to you later."

"Bye!" Rayna hung up the phone and stared at it for a minute. She knew Sam was probably writing at that time in the afternoon, but he would want to know about the radium on the mountain. She needed to call Fieldman, and fill him in, too. It occurred to her that she also needed to do more research on tritium and radium and look at that report again.

"Okay," she thought. "I'll call Sam and get him to meet me for dinner. Then I'll fill Fieldman in, and then I'll get that research done. She moved from her softer chair to the stiff backed, more formal one behind the computer desk. Rest could come later. There was too much to do.

Sam was not only willing to have dinner with Rayna, he even stopped and picked her up to take her to the "good diner." There were only two in town, right across the street from each other. Everyone had his favorite. Theirs was the one with the newer booths, the friendlier waitresses, and the root beer floats.

Gina always greeted them with a warm smile and a happy voice. "Hi, Miss Rayna and Mr. Sam! How are you tonight?" She pointed them in the direction of a clean booth as she wiped the counter.

"We're fine, just fine," Sam answered.

"Busy as ever," Rayna answered, "and you?"

"I'm just peachy!" She sang. "You two just have a seat, and I'll be right over to take your order."

Sam and Rayna sat in the back-corner booth, where they preferred to be. It was a little more private, and they had confidential matters to discuss. Gina tended to her customers the way she would want to be treated if she were one. She took their orders, served them, and then said, "holler if you need anything else." She never hovered and rarely interrupted a conversation. Yet, she would still be there with a refill or an extra napkin the moment it was needed. Gina was really the best reason of all to eat at the good diner.

"The suspense is killing me, Rayna" Sam said eagerly. "What did you find? What did Vincent find? Why did you have to go all the way up to Bell to talk to the ranger? Wouldn't a phone call have worked?" That last question was a jab. He knew she normally would have called if she didn't really want to see someone on a busy work day.

Rayna ignored half of his questions. "Okay, our friend, the professor had some interesting findings at the farm and on the mountain." Rayna filled him in on the soil composition reports, emphasizing where the tritium was found at the farm and where the radium was found in the triangle on the mountain. "And here's the weird thing," she said finishing her summary, "Lee's symptoms sound like radiation poisoning, and his car was found near where we found unusually high levels of radium."

Sam's countenance was hard to read. His eyes were bright, but his brow showed concern. "I can't decide if that's a good thing, or a bad thing," he said. "I mean, of course, radiation poisoning is a bad thing, but doesn't that put him up there on the mountain with his car?"

"I don't know. It's hard to say when he got separated from the Mustang. He wouldn't do it willingly, that's for sure. He loves that car."

"Where else could he have gotten the…" Sam's words trailed off as Gina walked up to refill their waters. "Thanks!" He nodded to her.

"No problem!" She walked away.

Rayna didn't let him finish his question. "If we are dealing with a UFO, he might have gotten the radiation poisoning, assuming that's what it is, on the UFO. He certainly didn't get it by rolling around in the grass on the mountain. There wasn't enough of it to affect him like that. At least, I don't think there was. The professor said it was really up to the rangers whether or not to cordon of the area for safety. The risk was relatively low."

"Did you talk to Fieldman?"

"Yes, and he's trying not to be too excited about this potentially being a full-blown *Close Encounters of the Third Kind* type case." Rayna looked back at Gina who was wiping down lunch menus. "We don't want anyone to know, right? If he gets all excited, he might decide to bring in other MUFON investigators. Most of them are trustworthy, but just like with people in the paranormal field, some don't care about confidentiality agreements like we do. They just want to post – in all of their excitement – whatever they find on the internet for all the world to see. They just want to make a name for themselves by saying 'look what I found!' We have to be cautious."

"Right. I agree. Let's keep this to ourselves until we know more. I think between a geologist, a meteorologist, a chemistry professor, and a ranger, we can handle this."

"And a writer," Rayna added.

"I'm trying to forget that I'm a writer for the moment. Like you said, we don't want this to get out. I'm going against everything I'm supposed to be doing for a living by sitting on this story."

"Thank you for that." Rayna waved at Gina and gave her the universal sign for "check please!"

Sam nodded in agreement toward Gina and continued. "This story is getting good, as far as stories go, because somebody has been put at risk. Lee still doesn't know what happened to him or why. We don't know if they were after him or your laptop."

"I know," Rayna felt that rush of guilt again and looked down at her empty plate. "I hate that."

"Here's the thing – and forgive me if I'm repeating myself like the big brother you never had: I want you to be careful! I know you live for this stuff, but you really have to keep your head about you. Sometimes you get so wrapped up in an investigation that you forget the basics like don't get too emotionally involved."

"I can't help it. I am here to help others."

"Do you know how many times that's gotten you into trouble?"

"Not *that* many." Rayna shrugged.

"Remember the time something pushed you into the wall in that theater we were investigating?"

Rayna lifted her hand and rubbed her neck. "Yeah, I had a knot on the back of my head for a week."

Sam continued, "What about the time that guy cornered you in his old, 'haunted' barn?"

Rayna giggled. "He had a knot on the back of his head for a week!"

"I'll give you that, but it wouldn't have happened if you weren't always so eager to help."

"But it's what I do!" She asserted.

"Uh-huh."

Gina interrupted momentarily with the check. "Here ya go, Sweetie. I'll take it up at the counter when you're ready."

"Thank you," Rayna replied. She turned her attention back to the argument at hand as soon as Gina was behind the counter again. "Okay, what about the clients who were at their wits' end in that trailer with no money and no one to stay with? Thanks to us, they're comfortable in their own home again. And that theater manager is finding it easier to keep employees since we cleared the building. Sure, I had a minor incident, but you have to admit that physical interaction with a ghost is pretty cool!"

"Yes, but not at your expense. You're too..."

"Reckless?" Rayna's face was starting to flush.

Sam motioned with his hands for her to calm down. "No, fearless!"

"Fearless is good. You can't be a paranormal investigator and be a scaredy-cat. You can't fear the dark, or a shadow, or the unknown. That's the whole point – to investigate the unknown!"

"True, but..."

"You're not going to tell me to be afraid..."

"Just have a little caution." Sam urged her.

"I do," her voice pleaded.

"A little more," Sam iterated.

"I'll think about it." Rayna conceded. "What time is it?"

Sam looked at his watch. "About quarter after seven," he answered.

"Ugh. It's too late to go by and visit Barb and Lee."

"Too late? It's only after seven! What are they, octogenarians?"

"Of course not," Rayna answered. "I just know that it's going to either be a very long visit or a very short visit, and I'm leaning toward long. Lee hasn't been sleeping. What if he actually is now? I'd hate to be the reason he misses his shut-eye."

"Lame excuse," Sam rolled his eyes. "You're not ready to face him, yet."

Rayna couldn't hide the truth from a man who'd known her almost all of her life. "You're right. I can't help it. I feel like I need to be strong and positive when I go talk to him, and I can't think about what happened and feel that way right now."

"He survived, didn't he?"

"Yes, but Barb says he's not the same." Rayna paused and lowered her eyes. "I'll call her and tell her I can't visit tonight. She'll understand. She knows me as well as you do."

Rayna made the call from the car as Sam drove her back to her house. It wasn't a long drive in a small town, but the phone call wasn't very long either. Rayna was ending the call when Sam pulled into her driveway. "That's odd," Rayna said.

"What?"

"The lamp is off."

"Did you leave it on?"

"I thought I did."

"You do have a ghost," Sam said in jest.

Rayna ignored him. "Um… why is Cloud sitting on the front porch?"

Chapter 12

The little black cat was pacing near the front door, flicking her tail back and forth in a show of irritation. She was looking inside the house and completely ignoring Rayna, who jumped out of Sam's car, slammed the passenger door and was running across her lawn to the front entry. Rayna paused only when she reached the door and heard Cloud growling that low growl that meant something was very wrong inside.

Rayna's screen door was tilted on its hinges and hanging open a few inches. She looked back at Sam who was walking up behind her. "What's wrong?" He asked.

"The door's open." Rayna scooped Cloud into her arms and kissed her forehead. The cat was still annoyed. "What happened, Cloud?" She whispered.

Inside the house, Raya heard something clatter like metal falling on wood. She turned and tossed the cat to Sam, who caught her reflexively. Cloud growled again, but Sam knew it wasn't directed at him. That little cat had always thought she was a guard dog. Rayna pulled the door open and it squeaked. "Who's in there?" she yelled and started to step inside.

"Wait!" Sam grabbed her arm. "What if whoever's in there is armed?"

Rayna looked into the darkness of her hallway directly in front of the door. "You let my cat out!" she called into the house. "I'm calling the police!" Then, Rayna looked back at Sam who had a quizzical look on his face. She shrugged. "What?" He chuckled despite himself. In the moment her eyes were fixed on Sam, she heard the backdoor slam. "Damn it!" she swore and ran inside. The back door was at the end of the hallway in front of her. She saw it bounce and shut again, but she couldn't see who was on the other side of it. She ran to that door and yelled for Sam to meet her in the backyard.

Sam dropped Cloud and did his best imitation of a sprinter around the side of the house. He was not a small man and was already winded by the time he met Rayna in the back. She was looking at the woods that backed up to her property. Despite her anger and curiosity, she decided not to follow the intruder. Instead she pulled out her phone and dialed 911.

Sam stood, legs spread, bent over, and still trying to catch his breath. "Did you see him?" he gasped.

"No." She frowned. "Not at all."

A voice answered her call, "911, what's your emergency?"

"My house was just broken into. The person isn't far. He just ran into the woods behind it."

"What's your address, ma'am?"

Rayna gave the operator her information and promised to wait outside. Sam offered to get his flashlight out of the car and go back into the woods to search for the guy, but Rayna said "no." Sam was right. They didn't know if the person was armed, or alone, for that matter.

Familiar faces in the forms of deputies showed up and swept the scene for evidence: fingerprints, footprints, and anything else that might have left a clue. They took photos and made notes, and then, finally, they let Rayna inside. She walked through the house slowly with a middle-aged, balding deputy named Ralph by her side. She noted what was out of place, and in her library, she knew exactly what was missing. Her desktop was still there, but the external back-up drive that sat next to it was gone. Her heart sank. What if the files on her desktop were missing? How could she run her business? She pushed her chair away from the desk and turned the computer on, but the deputy stopped her cold. "I'm sorry, Miss Rayna. If the drive is missing, we're going to have to dust the computer and the desk for prints. You can't touch anything else in here."

Sam walked up beside her, and gently pulled her away. She was speechless. He told her quietly, "Let's let them do what they're here to do, and then we'll see if everything's where it should be." Then, he led her back outside where Cloud was sitting on the front porch, still looking a bit peeved. "The lock on the front door is broken," he said. "It's not safe to stay here tonight."

"They won't be back," she said, not raising her eyes from the ground. "They got what they were after."

"What's on your computers that's so damned important?"

"I wish I knew." She paused for a moment. "All of my client files, weather forecasts, historical data, business stuff... and all of my research into the stuff surrounding our cases."

"Including this one?"

"Especially this one. My focus is usually ghosts, not UFO's and radiation poisoning. I've been doing a ton of research. The professor's soil results were on that drive, too."

Sam frowned. "So, the question is whether this is related to that case, or if it's corporate espionage."

Rayna looked up at her friend. "No one wants my business except maybe Kate, and she has access to all of that stuff when she comes over to work. She's got no reason to break the lock. She has a key. Nobody else around here gives a damn about the weather forecasting business unless the TV met gets it very wrong."

"So, it's definitely about this case," Sam concluded.

"Nothing's definite, but that would be my assumption."

There was a long pause in the conversation and Rayna sat down on the porch floor next to her cat. Sam watched her pick the cat up, rub her behind the ear, and whisper to her. "You're coming to stay with me for a while," he finally said.

"No…"

"Yes." He insisted. "Just until we know it's safe."

"What about Cloud?"

"She can come, too. Just call Kate and offer her some overtime. Tell her whatever you need to tell her without saying too much. If she takes it, then that will free you up to spend more time figuring this out. The sooner we're done with this one, the better. I don't like thinking what might have happened if you had been here tonight."

Rayna held Cloud a little closer to her chest, and put her chin on the cat's head. Cloud purred loudly. "I don't want to intrude."

"Shut up." Sam said curtly. "It's not an intrusion. I insist… unless, of course, you want to call your sister or mother and explain all of this?"

"Not really."

"And Barb has Lee at her house, and you're not staying here until the locks are fixed and we feel more sure that whomever we frightened away tonight is not coming back."

Rayna sighed. "Fine. I guess I should say 'thank you.'"

"You're welcome." Sam forced a smile.

Chapter 13

Just two days had passed since the break-in, and Sam was already out of food. "I'm sorry. I'm not used to shopping for more than just me," he told Rayna as they walked into their favorite diner for breakfast. Gina was behind the counter with a smile, and a carafe of freshly brewed coffee in hand. Sam pointed at it and asked, "Is that for me?".

"It is if you want it!" She followed Sam and Rayna to a table and wiped it down for them. "The morning rush came early today."

"A morning rush in Jupiter?" Rayna asked.

"Yeah, there are some new faces around lately. I don't know if it's just that new bed and breakfast down the highway, or what's going on, but it's all good. Fresh blood, ya know?" Gina smiled and sat the coffee pot down on the table. "It helps if I get some mugs, huh?" Before they could answer, she had walked away.

"New bed and breakfast?" Sam repeated. "I don't remember hearing about a new bed and breakfast."

"Me either." Rayna said.

Gina was back, "Oh, I didn't either. These two nice lookin' guys were just here this morning. I asked where they were from and they were kind of sketchy with their answer. 'The city' they said. So, I asked why they were visiting, and they said they were just passing through. I asked where they were staying, and they said the new B&B up the street. I just figured I had missed out on that one."

Gina was already writing on her server's pad. "Do you want the usual, Mr. Sam?"

"Yes, please." Sam's grin was as big as the Chesire cat's.

"Miss Rayna?"

"I'll have the French toast, please."

Gina nodded and walked away.

"There's no new bed and breakfast up the road." A voice from behind Sam said. Sam twisted around in his seat to see who had been eaves dropping. He recognized Ralph, the deputy that had helped two nights before at Rayna's house. He was dressed in plain clothes – khakis and a blue polo shirt – and was sitting across the table from a middle-aged woman with ash colored hair peeking out from under a baseball cap.

"Oh, hi there, Deputy." Sam reached his hand around to shake Ralph's. "Day off?"

"Yeah. Thought I'd treat my wife to breakfast for a change." He motioned to the woman across the table, who smiled shyly.

"So, no new bed and breakfast?" Rayna didn't bother with pleasantries before coffee.

"No, ma'am," Ralph answered. "I don't know of any nearby, and you know the Sheriff's office would know about something like that. I can't figure why they'd lie about it though."

"Did you see these guys?" Sam asked.

"Yes. They were finishing up while we were getting started. I heard 'em talking to Gina and being kind of round-about with their answers. My ears perked up a bit. She was just trying to make small talk with 'em, but they weren't real talkative. I may not be on duty today, but I'm always on if ya know what I mean." He gestured widely as if to point out the whole of the town. "It's what I do."

Rayna caught a glimpse of Ralph's wife shaking her head and smiled. "I bet you've got your thumb on the pulse of this county."

"I try, ma'am. We live here, too, ya know. I've got to keep my homeland safe."

Sam nodded his head. "So what did these strangers look like?"

"Nicely dressed. They were both wearing black suits. Had their sunglasses on inside like they were from Hollywood or something. Of course, the sun comes in pretty strong through those windows in the morning. Maybe they were just protecting their eyes." He looked back at his wife and pointed at her. "She thought they were government men, but I told her we would know if some outside agency were poking around our jurisdiction. I'm guessing they were boyfriends on a road trip."

Rayna nearly spit her coffee out. "Boyfriends?" She choked. "Really? Why?"

"Straight men don't dress in suits for a drive through the mountains."

Sam chuckled at the thought. "No, no, I guess they probably don't."

Ralph and his wife stood up to leave. Ralph shook Sam's hand again and nodded at Rayna. "Miss Rayna, if you want to stop by the Sheriff's office later, the Sheriff will be there. He'd like to see ya, I'm sure. Then you could pick up your copy of the burglary report in case you need it for insurance reasons."

"Thanks, Ralph. I'll probably do that after breakfast."

"He probably won't be in until closer to noon, but whatever works for your schedule is fine." Ralph nodded again, took his wife by the hand, and left the diner.

"Hm..." Sam wondered out loud. "Strangers in dark suits and shades, huh?"

Rayna shook her head. "Don't even go there."

"It was bound to happen," her friend said. "Don't you see?"

"No, Sam."

"Yes, you do." He nodded his head in an exaggerated motion. "Yes, you do!"

"We do not have MIB running around in Jupiter."

"By definition and description, I think we just might."

"No, Sam." Rayna repeated.

"We shall see, now, won't we?" He sat back in his seat and folded his arms just in time for Gina to arrive with their breakfast plates.

The American flag folded over onto itself as it swayed gently in the breeze. The low, bulky cumulus clouds that moved in after breakfast and were broken up by slivers of sunshine were its backdrop. Rayna sat in her truck watching it and fighting the urge to close her eyes.

Sleep wasn't coming easily lately. Between the case, concern over her business, and the break-in, she had a hard time relaxing. Sleeping on Sam's couch wasn't exceedingly comfortable, but at least, it felt safer than her own. Living alone had never bothered her until now. She hated this new feeling of insecurity.

Sam, the old dear, protective friend that he was, was being very supportive about the whole thing. He had insisted Rayna stay at his place until the police had a lead or a reason not to tie the break-in to Lee's disappearance. Sam didn't want Rayna at home alone. Even Cloud was welcome at his place.

Rayna knew she couldn't sleep on his couch forever. Whether her friends in the Sheriff's office cracked the case or not, she had to go home eventually. Fieldman had offered up his couch, too, and Barb said, "a sleepover would be fun! Like old times!" Rayna just didn't like to feel like a burden or a pity case. No, she made her mind up. She was sleeping in her own bed that night.

A tap on her driver's side window startled her. She didn't realize her eyes had closed. It was Wolf, and he was smiling at her. That was a pleasant sight to wake to. Rayna rolled down the window.

"Want some company?" he asked.

She unlocked the truck doors. "Come on in."

He walked around to the passenger side and got in. "How are you doing?"

"Okay." She forced a grin. Smiling at Wolf shouldn't have been difficult, but the reason behind the innocent question made her unhappy.

"Really?" He didn't seem to believe her.

"Sure."

"Well you look a little tired. Did I just catch you sleeping in your car?"

"No."

"No?"

"I think I was just resting my eyes." She rubbed them without thinking.

"For how long?"

Rayna looked at the clock on her dash board and considered it. "Huh. Probably longer than I thought."

"Please tell me you didn't sleep in your truck last night." Wolf looked around and behind the seat for some sign of a campout in the vehicle.

"I did not." She rubbed her eyes again. "I slept on Sam's couch."

"How'd that go?"

"Not very well. I'm a very light sleeper, even in my own bed. Poor Cloud stayed cuddled up near me all night. I was afraid I'd roll over and squish her. I'm not used to sleeping with..." She stopped, realizing what she was about to say.

"With?" Wolf asked.

"Another living being, I guess." Rayna blushed a little and looked down at her lap. Wolf was attractive enough to make her nervous and very aware of double entendre.

"I expected you to say 'cat'!" He laughed.

"I think the word I was going to use was 'anyone.'" She laughed, too. "Yep! I'm tired and the brain is not functioning well."

"So, how long do you plan on using Sam's couch?"

She shook her head. "Not long. I need to go home. I want to be back in my own space."

"Do you think it's safe?"

"I don't know. That's the problem. I don't know who it was, or what they wanted, or if they found it, or whether they'll return. We have dead horses falling from the sky, a disappearing/reappearing IT guy, a missing computer, a break-in, a missing backup drive..." Her voice trailed off.

"I know."

"I don't know if it's all connected, or just random coincidence. There are too many questions and not enough answers."

The two sat in silence for a minute pondering the questions. Rayna stared out through the windshield. Wolf watched her, but he couldn't tell if she was as stressed as he expected a woman in her situation to be. She seemed very calm, cool, and collected under the circumstances. Jess would have been a neurotic mess by now.

Jess... oh, yeah. He thought about the blind date that had turned into a reluctant relationship of sorts. More like sordid. He still had to decide how to end that. It wasn't that he didn't like her. She was pretty and a good cook. The problem was that he just liked her. He never felt any real connection to her. It wasn't fair for him to continue to see her when she obviously wanted more.

In the meantime, Wolf sat beside a woman who impressed him on many levels, and on some, she even perplexed him. She was educated as a scientist, but immersed in New Age beliefs. She appeared fearless to the world, but was obviously not immune to concern for her own safety. She quit a comfortable job on television to start her own business and live in a small town. She could be a local celebrity, but she preferred to be incognito.

Wolf looked at Rayna and noticed that her eyes were closed again. Then, through the window, he saw the sheriff enter the building in front of them. He tapped her gently on the shoulder, and she opened her eyes, looked at him and smiled. "Sorry," she said.

Wolf pointed to the building, "The Sheriff is here."

"Okay. Good then." Rayna rubbed her eyes once more and opened the truck door. "Let's go."

The Sheriff was already busy behind a closed office door when Wolf and Rayna entered the county building. Barb was behind her desk facing the entrance and grinned broadly when she saw the two arriving together. "So," she asked in a chipper voice, "what's on the agenda for today?"

"I need to pick up my report from the other night," Rayna answered.

"I think she needs a nap, too." Wolf added.

Barb flashed Rayna a shocked look, one eyebrow raised. "Oh, really?"

Rayna shot back a look that said, "Shut up, Barb!", but her voice said, "Sam's couch isn't that comfy with me and a cat sharing it."

Barb sank back in her chair a little. "Oh."

"Is the Sheriff available?" Rayna glanced at his closed door. "I think he might want to be filled in on the Lovell case."

"He does," Barb acknowledged, "but he's got somebody in there with him. I think he's from the Capital. He doesn't want to be interrupted."

"Okay," Wolf said. "Will he be free later?" Barb nodded and grinned at the handsome ranger. "So, then… maybe lunch is on the agenda?"

"I'd love to!" Barb answered. Rayna glared at her, but Barb paid no attention to her. "Where should we go? The diner, or the other diner?"

Wolf laughed. "How about the other diner?"

"Well, since I was just at the diner for breakfast, the other diner for lunch makes sense." Rayna said.

"Oh, you're coming too?" Barb winked at her friend, and Rayna nearly growled.

"Tell you what," Wolf said, "I'll buy."

"Really?" Barb asked. "Let me grab my purse!" She was around the desk in a beat. "I'm not one to pass up a free meal from a handsome man."

Rayna agreed. "She's not one to pass up a free meal or a handsome man."

Wolf just shook his head. "Do you want to drive or walk?"

"Let's walk," Rayna answered. "I could use the fresh air to clear my head."

The diners weren't far from the county building, just a few short blocks. Wolf walked in between Rayna and Barb, who kept looking around him at her friend and making faces. Rayna loved Barb, but it sometimes felt like they'd never left high school. She could be so childish. Still, it was nice to see her friend enjoying herself for a change. It had been a week since she had acted a little carefree with all of the drama in their lives lately. Rayna hated drama.

They were just rounding the corner leading to the restaurant when a tall woman with tanned skin, chocolate brown hair, and perfectly plucked eyebrows nearly bumped into them. She looked like she was on a mission. To Rayna's surprise, the woman grabbed Wolf by the arm and pulled him a few feet away from them. Wolf appeared surprised. Barb froze, shocked. "We need to talk!" the stranger demanded.

Nothing good ever comes from conversations that start with "we need to talk." Rayna knew it, Barb knew it, and by the look on his face, Wolf knew it, too. His entire demeanor changed when he saw Jess march toward him when they turned that corner. Her jaw was tight, and her eyes narrowed. "She'd be pretty if she weren't so angry," Rayna thought to herself.

Jess was quite striking actually. No one in her town actually knew what her ethnic make-up was. Fifty years ago, that would have made her an outcast in a rural southern town, but today it made her beautiful. Yet, her face was tight with emotion, and her arms were crossed as she stood there with Wolf.

She had taken him several steps away from Rayna and Barb, but not out of earshot. Barb wondered if she meant to make this argument – what was looking like a break-up – public, or if she just couldn't judge how close they were. Rayna turned to face Barb, who was standing, blatantly staring at Wolf and Jess. Rayna put both hands on Barb's shoulder and turned her so that they were facing each other. "They don't need an audience," Rayna whispered to her friend.

"Oh," Barb quietly replied, "I think they do."

"Let's not make it painfully obvious," Rayna half-agreed. She could tell Barb's ears weren't hearing a word she said while Jess was telling Wolf how unhappy she was with their current arrangement.

Rayna watched out of the corner of her eye. Wolf's body language was not that of a man being dumped. He had lost the deer-caught-in-headlights look. Meanwhile, Jess seemed to go from angry to relieved. Yes, relieved. She had to get her feelings off her chest, and as she ran out of steam, her jaw relaxed. She wasn't done, yet, though. Wolf had not tried to argue or defend himself. He stood there quietly and let her rant fall over him and roll off his shoulders. He almost looked immune to her barrage of words.

"I don't want to be your good time girl," Rayna heard Jess say. "I want to be your anytime girl... and maybe someday, your all time girl." Wolf kept mum. "When you close your eyes at night and you're alone and you think about the meaning of life and of love, who comes to your mind?" Her voice was now pleading. He stared at her for a moment and then turned his eyes toward the sidewalk beneath him. "It's not me, is it?" She demanded.

"No," he answered quietly without looking up.

Jess sighed. "I guess I'm not surprised." Tears welled up in her eyes, and her voice started to shake a little. "I think I'm done here."

"Jess…" Wolf finally looked at her again.

"We're done." Jess said with resolve.

"I'm sorry."

"I'm sure." She held herself together as she walked away from him.

Rayna stood in silence, feeling sorry for Jess. She knew what it was like to fall for someone who didn't feel the same way. Still, Wolf had been honest with her all along, so there was a limit to Rayna's sympathy. Her thoughts were interrupted by a light tap on her arm. Barb was making sure Rayna saw Wolf look at her as he turned away from Jess's retreat. Rayna couldn't decipher the look when their eyes met. Was it shame? Embarrassment? Or something else?

Wolf averted his eyes momentarily and then looked back at the pair of friends. "I'm sorry you had to witness that."

"It was a little awkward," Barb admitted.

"No problem," Rayna said softly. Wolf's eyes were searching her face for something. "What?" She finally asked.

"Nothing," he said and looked down at his shoes. "I've… um… got to go."

"You do?" Barb asked. "I thought you were going to…"

"Sorry. I owe you both lunch, but I can't now."

Rayna nodded understandingly, and he walked past them and back toward the Sheriff's office.

"It's you," Barb whispered.

"What?" Rayna asked without taking her eyes of the ranger as he walked away.

"It's you, Rayna. Don't you see?" Barb pointed at Wolf. "You're the one he thinks about. You're the one she wanted to be."

"No," Rayna couldn't believe what Barb was saying. "No."

"Yes!" Barb was dancing around her like a little girl. "Yes, yes, yes!"

"No, Barb, it can't be."

"And why not?" she stood still and crossed her arms.

"Because it's *never* me."

Chapter 14

Lunch at the other diner had been bland and uneventful, which was a pleasant change from the pre-lunch walk to the diner. Rayna kept Barb off the subject of Wolf and talked about Lee instead. The two decided that it was time for Rayna to pay him a visit that evening. She hoped to help him recall some of his missing time by getting him to relax a little more than he'd been able to since the incident.

The duo was returning to the county building when a man approached them on the sidewalk. His face was round, and his cheeks drooped a little like an English bulldog's. Their weight seemed to pull the corners of his lips down in a permanent frown. He had an unlit cigarette dangling from that sad mouth, and his beady eyes looked at Rayna intently.

"May we help you?" Barb demanded, sensing Rayna's uneasiness at the realization that the man was staring her down.

"I doubt it," the man finally answered in a low, deep grumble, never taking his eyes off Rayna and not even bothering to blink. Although, it unnerved her, Rayna met his stare. She searched his eyes for a purpose and let her psychic guard down. The word "incredible" came to mind. Then an image flashed briefly in front of her: bright lights over a field.

Rayna steeled her nerves and let the words come. "Are you wondering what you've seen?"

The man blinked twice and the dangling cigarette fell from its precarious perch on his lower lip. He snapped out of his frozen position and bent down to pick it up. Rayna noticed the large, bald spot on the back of his head and red marks on his neck. When he straightened up, he looked as if he'd just woken from a dream. The man sighed and said, "I think I know what it was."

Barb stared at her friend. Rayna took a deep breath and asked, "when was it?"

"Last month," the man answered slowly. "How did you know?"

"Lucky guess," Rayna replied. "Where were you?"

"I was on the road, about a mile from my house, not too far from that horse farm where the animal died."

"How did you know about that?" Barb interrupted. Without thinking, Rayna raised her hand and motioned Barb not to interrupt. Barb obeyed.

"It's a small town. People talk." The round-faced man answered. "I've told no one."

"You're right," Rayna told the man. "I probably can't help you, but I can listen if you need to talk."

The man gave a small nod. Then he answered, "I think I'd rather just forget it," and he turned and walked away slowly.

Barb stared after him. "How did you know?" she asked.

Rayna answered simply, "I saw what he was thinking."

Barb looked back at her friend. "That's almost scary." A smile crept across her face. "Quick! What am I thinking?"

Rayna paused and laughed. "I cannot discuss that in public!"

Changing the subject, Barb said, "You know that new deputy? The cute one?"

"Yes."

"He asked if he could take me to dinner tonight."

"Are you going?"

"No. You're coming over to talk to Lee, remember?" Barb answered.

"I am, but I can come over after dinner, or I could talk with him while you're out."

"No," Barb insisted, "I want to be there for him."

"Then go to dinner, and I'll meet you at your place at 7:00."

"I guess that will work," Barb agreed.

"I'm glad you're going." Rayna told her. "It's good to see you getting back into things. You worry me when you're not having fun."

"I should worry you when I am having fun!"

Rayna laughed again and gave her friend a side-ways hug as they approached Rayna's car. "At least I know when you're having fun that you're having a good day. You go have fun after work, and I'll see you tonight."

Rayna pulled into Barb's driveway at exactly 7:00pm. She prided herself on punctuality. Unfortunately, sometimes Barb lost track of time and was a little late to her own parties, so Rayna wasn't surprised to see a patrol car pull into the drive behind her. In her rear-view mirror, she watched the young, red-haired deputy exit his side of the vehicle, walk around the car and open Barb's door for her. He walked her to her front porch and proceeded to plant a big kiss on her lips. Barb threw her arms around his neck and kissed him back, and the make-out session began.

Rayna tried not to watch. The couple was oblivious to their audience, and she really didn't want to intrude on their privacy. Still, after several minutes, Rayna decided she was done being respectful. Barb could go on all night like that. It was great, Rayna thought, that Barb was back to being Barb, but it wasn't great that Rayna was sitting in her truck waiting for the kissing to stop.

Barb didn't notice Rayna's truck door slam, but the deputy did. He snapped to attention, when Rayna approached the porch. Barb was wiping her lips with her shirt sleeve.

"At ease," Rayna joked. "I hate to interrupt a good time, but…"

"I was just leaving, ma'am," the young deputy assured her. He turned to Barb and smiled. "I'd like to see you again, Barbara," he said softly.

"I think that can be arranged." Barb answered with a grin, and with that, he turned, skipped the stairs leading off the porch and was back to his car in a flash.

Rayna watched him leave with a silly, school-boy look on his face, and then looked at her friend beside her. "Wow! That was… impressive."

"You're just jealous."

"No, I'm pretty sure I'm not. Not very much anyway."

"Rayna, you really need to take the opportunities when they arise!" Barb chided her. "You know how hard it is to meet new guys in this little town. Take the chance while you have it! Go after Wolf!"

"How the heck did your little make-out session on the porch become about me?"

Barb folded her arms in mock anger. "It's always about you, my dear!"

Rayna took a deep breath and shook her head. "No, right now, it's about Lee." She pointed at the door. "Shall we?"

"Let's." Barb agreed.

Barb sat in her recliner, and Lee was lying on the couch as comfortably as he could make himself. His face looked less burned, but it was still a little more pink than usual. Rayna sat in a club chair facing the couch. Lee was taking deep breaths the way Rayna had instructed him. His eyes were closed, and his hands were folded over his stomach. Barb watched silently for a moment, and then spoke up. "Wait a minute. You're going to hypnotize him, right? Before we do this, did you hear about that guy Benny at the hardware store?"

"No," Rayna shook her head.

Barb continued, "He went to one of those hypnotist comedians and was called up on stage. He said nothing happened, but now anytime he hears the word 'smack' he slaps himself in the face."

"No kidding!" Lee's eyes were open again.

"It wouldn't be a problem if he weren't such a wrestling fan," Barb said.

Rayna didn't understand. "Huh?"

Barb explained, "You know WWE Smackdown? Every week he watches reruns and slaps himself silly!"

Rayna shook her head and stifled a giggle. Lee just stared at his sister in disbelief.

"Lee," Rayna said. "I'm not really going to hypnotize you, and I'm not here to make jokes. You know that right?" Lee nodded at her. "Good, then forget the craziness Barb just told us, and close your eyes again. We're just going to help you relax, or I am anyway."

Barb sat still and became silent again. Lee closed his eyes and laid back on the couch and took a few more deep breaths. After a few minutes, Rayna spoke. "What's the last thing you remember that night?"

Lee answered in almost a whisper, "After my date, I was pulling into my driveway and thinking that I had to get your laptop out of the back."

Rayna was slightly incredulous, but kept her voice even. "That's really the last thing you remember?"

"Yes, it really is."

Barb interjected, "Lee, really. Relax, okay?"

"I am," Lee took another deep breath. "I'm trying to anyway." He glared at his sister.

"You're not." She insisted. "I can tell by your posture and your eyes that you are not relaxed."

Lee sighed deeply.

"Take another deep breath," Rayna said. "Close your eyes, and let it go slowly. Keep your eyes closed and take another deep breath. Feel your chest expand and fill with air. Now release that air slowly and be mindful of how it feels as it escapes your lungs." Rayna watched Lee sink deeper into the couch. "Now keep your eyes closed just a little longer and keep breathing deeply. Slow, deep breaths." Lee's eyelids lost the wrinkles around them as his face relaxed.

When Rayna was confident, he was as comfortable as he was going to get, she said, "now keep your eyes closed and think about that night again. When you pulled into your driveway, what did you see?"

"My house," Lee answered.

"Did anything about your house seem out of place?"

"No."

"What about the yard?"

"It's all normal," he said quietly.

"What do you see in the yard?"

Lee took a deep breath. "Bushes, grass needs mowing, neighbor's dog running away."

Rayna thought for a minute. "Running away or running toward something?" she asked.

There was a long pause as Lee took more deep breaths. "Away," he finally answered, "with his tail between his legs."

"What was he running away from?"

"Don't know." Lee answered.

"Okay, keep your eyes closed and keep breathing big, deep breaths. What's going on behind your car?"

"Nothing."

"Nothing at all?" Rayna questioned.

"Not behind me."

"Is there anything beside your car?"

"No."

"What about above you?"

"There's a helicopter."

"A helicopter?" Barb whispered.

Lee continued, "The light's getting brighter like it's getting closer."

"Can you hear it coming?" Rayna asked.

There was a long pause, and Lee answered "no." He opened his eyes. "No. No! I never heard it."

"How close did it come?" Rayna asked as she gestured with her hands for him to stay calm.

"It was right over me."

"Did you watch it fly away?"

Lee closed his eyes for a moment. "I don't... I don't know." His voice was tight and he was breathing faster.

"It's okay, Lee." Rayna assured him.

"No!" His voice panicked, "I don't remember anything after that. I looked up. It was above me. There was no sound. Then... *nothing*!"

"I think we're probably done here." Barb stood from her chair and walked to sit on the edge of the couch next to Lee.

"I think you're right," Rayna agreed. She felt helpless for her old friends. "I'm sorry, Hon," she told him. "My goal was to help you remember, not stress you even more."

"It's not your fault," Lee said. "I just can't... can't..."

"Shh..." Barb held his hand. "It's okay."

"No," he said, his voice tight with fear. "It's not okay. It's not. I can't remember what happened. I can't remember two days of my life. One minute there was a light, and the next, I'm in a hospital being told they'd found my family and you were on the way to get me. Me! All the way in Knoxville! What the hell was I doing in Knoxville?"

Rayna didn't know what to say. She just sat in silence and wished she hadn't come to Barb's that night.

Barb turned to look at her and nodded toward the door. "I don't think we should keep talking about this." Lee sat up and buried his head in his sister's shoulder. "Do you mind?" She asked Rayna.

Rayna whispered an apology, and walked slowly toward the door. Her eyes were filling with tears for her friends. "I'll call you tomorrow," she said, and let herself out.

Chapter 15

Rayna left Barb's house with her mind in disarray. Lee had been able to recall more than she expected, but there was still a gaping hole of more than a day in his memory, and what he did remember seemed very disturbing. Rayna feared her friend had more sleepless nights ahead. Worse, she feared that she had made things worse for him by helping him recall the night he disappeared. The brain has a way of defending its owner by shutting out the harmful memories. There must be a reason Lee's had been repressed so quickly. Not being trained in psychology other than taking a class as an elective in college, Rayna was realizing her actions, although they were in an effort to help her friend, might have been reckless.

She and Barb had expected the name or some other identifier of Lee's kidnapper. Instead, they had more questions and an even more freaked out Lee. Rayna decided that she would offer to pay for professional therapy for her friend if he wanted it. She also swore at herself for dabbling in something that she had not been trained for, and then she swore to herself that she would never do that again.

There are times in life when, if someone told you an unbelievable story, you would dismiss it as exaggeration. In her avocation, Rayna had many of those moments. Unfortunately, recently, the unbelievable stories were her own, or that of her friends. She couldn't dismiss them. In fact, now that she was experiencing the situations herself, she was wondering how many others that she had previously taken with a grain of salt had actually warranted more of her attention. Years of personal encounters told to her by potential clients raced through her head as did a bit of regret for having prided herself on her healthy dose of skepticism when listening to them.

Rayna was pulling into her driveway when she saw a flash of lightning. There had only been a very slight chance for rain that evening, so she was a big surprised to see it. She stopped the truck engine and sat in silence waiting for the thunder to follow. Nothing. The lightning seemed close enough for the familiar sound to travel with it, but maybe she had misjudged the proximity.

There was another flash as she put her house key into the new lock on her side door. The front door had been replaced by a helpful neighbor the day before, and she had been to the house before she went to Barb's to clean it up and move Cloud back in. Rayna was happy to know she'd be sleeping in her own bed again. She did what she could to push the concern over another break-in as far back in her mind as possible.

Inside, Cloud purred at her from her favorite windowsill in the kitchen. Rayna poured the little cat a bowl of dry food and gave her permission to dig in. Then Rayna walked through the house, turning every light on and looking things over carefully. All of the windows were locked, the back door was locked, the new front door was locked, and everything else seemed in place. Even Grumpy's room appeared in perfect, untouched condition. Satisfied that she was safe again in the house she walked back through to turn all the lights back off.

When she reached the kitchen doorway, there was another flash outside. Instead of thunder, Rayna heard the sound of electricity ceasing: the wind down of motors humming and then silence. The power was out. "Damn!" Rayna cursed and walked over to the kitchen counter next to the sink. She always kept a flashlight within reach. She turned it on and walked down the dark hallway to the breaker box near the back door. Nothing was tripped. She glanced at the door's lock with an ounce of trepidation, but it was just as it had been a minute before – locked and secure.

Rayna walked back toward the front of the house and grabbed her cell phone from her purse. Then she looked out her front windows. The street light down on the corner about 100 yards from her house was dark. The few neighbors' houses she could see on her edge of town were also dark. She felt better knowing that it wasn't just her house that was plunged into silence.

She tried connecting to the internet to get the phone number for the power company online, but her smart phone wouldn't connect. After a few minutes of frustration, she took her flashlight into the office and dug out an old power bill. She was thankful she'd held on to it since she had been paying all of her bills online for years. The number connected and after pushing one several times on the keypad, a friendly voice picked up.

"Tennessee power. May I help you?"

"Hi, I need to report a power outage."

"Yes, ma'am. Where is the outage?"

"It's on the northeast side of Jupiter. At least, from what I can see it is. There aren't any lights on here on this side of town."

"I see. It looks like we've had a few calls from Jupiter. We have crews on the way."

"How long do you think this will last?"

"I can't say. I'm not sure if the cause has been diagnosed yet."

"Okay. Thank you." Rayna didn't wait for a response. She just hung up the phone and stared at it for a minute. Cloud walked to her and rubbed against her leg with a grateful purr. "I guess we ought to be thankful for the rare silence, Storm Cloud, and just go to bed." The cat seemed to agree and ran down the hallway ahead of her to Rayna's bedroom.

Rayna texted Sam, "I'm going to bed way early tonight. The cable and internet are out with the power. On top of that, my phone can't connect online. Now it's just a cell phone. I guess the alien invasion as begun. LOL." Adding the "lol" at the end didn't lessen the feeling that she might not be joking as much as she'd like to be. Without access to the solar monitors, satellite or radar feeds, she felt like a sitting duck.

She waited for Sam's reply, hoping for confirmation that he was without internet also, but none came. "What if texting doesn't work, either?" she thought. "I'm screwed." There was a momentary lapse of reason and an unusual sense of dread crept over her. "Get it together," she told herself, trying to shake it off. "The truck still works and Cloud is calm." Rayna looked at her cat curled up on the bed next to her. Cloud was her paranormal barometer, and she looked as peaceful as she could be under the circumstances. What does a cat care if the power is out?

Rayna took a deep breath to clear her mind and fend off a rare panic attack. "One too many sci-fi movies," she said to Cloud. "Stop letting me watch those things." The kitty just looked up at her and yawned.

The sound of her phone's text message alert startled her. She picked it up. Sam's response was "G'night." Apparently, he wasn't worried.

Rayna tried to remember a time when being disconnected wasn't unnerving. It was at least a decade ago. She reminded herself that life before the current communication technology was probably better with less stress, less in-demand-all-the-time feelings, and less instant gratification. She tried to think of the outage as a chance to unplug - a short vacation like the one she kept threatening to take.

This time it was the phone's ring that startled her. "Hello?" she answered quickly.

"Rayna?" It was Wolf.

"This is Rayna. Hi, Wolf, what's up?"

"Where are you right now?"

"At home on my bed."

"Can you go outside and look toward Bell Mountain?" His voice had a hint of something in it, but Rayna couldn't pinpoint the feeling.

Rayna stood up and walked to the front door. "Can I ask why?" She unlocked and opened the heavy door and looked out through the screened door, hesitant to step outside.

"There's something going on up here, and I just want to know if you can see anything from where you are."

Rayna stepped out onto the front porch. "Hang on. I'm going out." She walked out into the yard and looked toward the mountain, but with all the trees in her yard, she couldn't see much. "I don't see anything but trees. What am I looking for?"

"Strange lights."

Rayna's hair stood on end. She rubbed her right arm with her free hand. "You're kidding, right?"

"No, I'm not." Wolf's voice was tense. "Another ranger and I have been standing in a clearing here watching lights dance over the mountain. There's no sound and no way they are helicopters, planes or anything I've ever seen."

"Do they act intelligent?" Rayna walked out into her street for a clearer view. Bell Mountain was some distance away, but tall enough to be seen from Jupiter in daylight. In darkness, however, it was hard to see much other than a few stars peeking out from behind the ever-moving clouds.

"Intelligent?" Wolf repeated. "Maybe."

"There are too many clouds for me to see." Rayna felt like she was missing out. She was a little jealous, but at the same time relieved. I'd check the radar, but my... I have no power or internet access. My part of Jupiter is having an outage."

"I know." He said. "I heard the whole valley went dark as far as that goes. At least your cell still works."

"Thank God for that!"

"Do you want to come up here?" His question was a bit of a surprise to her.

"Um..."

"I think you'll want to see this."

"What if it stops before I get there?"

"I'll call you and tell you to turn around."

Rayna looked at the clouds again in the direction of the mountain and sighed. "Yeah, where are you on the mountain?"

"Where we found Lee's car."

Rayna felt another chill.

The road to Bell Mountain seemed longer than usual. Rayna split her attention between the road and the sky. The low cloud deck was showing some breaks here and there, but the mountain was still hard to see. She had to keep reminding herself to watch for deer on the empty stretch. Occasionally drivers would report seeing bear along the roadside, too. She wandered what other creatures might be watching from the dark woods.

The air that night seemed spiked with uneasiness. It wasn't normal for scary thoughts to flash through her mind. Even with all of the investigations she'd done, she rarely felt fear, anxiety, or had nightmares. She told herself that tonight's sensation was because the situation was not her norm. UFOs and freakish horse deaths may be beyond normal, but they were not part of her prior experience. She turned her truck up the windy road to the parking lot. Between the treetops above the road to her left, she saw a quick flash of light out of the corner of her eye. She slowed the truck and lowered the window. She couldn't hear any noise over the hum of her own engine. Rayna searched the sky for something more. She averted her eyes back to the road just in time to glimpse movement on the right shoulder. She stopped the pickup.

The headlights showed nothing in front of her, so she hit her brighter high beams. Still nothing. Just when she started to convince herself that it was either an animal or her imagination getting the better of her, she glimpsed shadowy motion again closer to the edge of the woods.

Rayna quickly grabbed her flashlight from her go-bag on the seat beside her and turned it on, pointing it in the direction for the movement. Rayna swept the light back and forth searching for an explanation. There was some glare from the light hitting the inside of the windshield, and her instinct told her to get out of the truck for a better look. Her nerves, surprisingly, kept her from doing it. Then, for a second, she saw a shadow in the trees. The shape looked human and not very tall. She froze and stared, but as quickly as she saw it, it disappeared. She moved the light from side to side, hoping to either recreate the shadow or see what caused it, but to no avail.

Rayna's phone's text message alert startled her. She put down the flashlight and grabbed the phone. "Where are you?" was the message from Wolf. She took a deep breath and looked back out the window toward the woods. "Almost there," she typed. Then, she put the truck in drive and drove the last half-mile to her destination.

Wolf and another ranger stood against his Jeep when Rayna pulled into the parking lot. The other ranger was shorter than Rayna, about 5 feet, 3 inches she guessed and had a conservative military haircut. He stayed near the Jeep as Wolf walked to Rayna's truck to open the door for her. "I was getting concerned. What took you so long?" He looked at her face. "Are you okay? You look a little pale."

"I'm fine." She looked at the other ranger. "I'll tell you later."

Wolf stepped aside to let Rayna pass and shut her door. There was a quick flash of light above them, and the other ranger yelled, "There!" and pointed above them. They both looked up in time to witness another flash. It was a quick burst of green light that streaked across a quarter of the sky above the tree line and faded fast.

"Is it a flare?" Rayna asked, still tilting her head back to see where it disappeared.

"I don't think so," the short-haired ranger answered.

There was a tinge of excitement in Wolf's voice. "We were hoping the meteorologist could help identify it."

"I see," Rayna said looking at the two of them. "Well, it definitely was *not* lightning."

"Not even ball lightning?" The other ranger asked.

Wolf suddenly remembered his manners. "Sorry, Rayna, this is Ranger Trace Cochran."

Trace stepped closer to her with his hand outstretched to shake hers. She took it firmly and smiled, "Nice to meet you, sir."

"Call me Trace. We were just out here about two hours ago when this started. We were talking about your friend that went missing and we found his car here. You know Mister..." his voice trailed off and he looked at his feet while searching for the name.

"My friend Lee." Rayna offered.

"Yeah, that's the one." The ranger seemed nervous and Rayna could feel his energy was all over the place. The excitement of the evening, or maybe too much coffee, had him wired. She was doing her best to stay grounded, especially after the weird event down the road, so she stepped a few feet back from him putting Wolf between the two of them as a buffer. She pretended that she needed a different view of the tree line and the sky while he spoke.

"So we're out here looking down, you know, at the ground for anything we might have missed, and I said 'Whoa! Was that lightning?' but there was no thunder. The next time it flashed, we looked up just in time to catch sight of one of those green... green..." Again, he was searching for what he wanted to say.

"Cheap fireworks?" Rayna offered.

"Is that what you think they are?" Trace asked.

Wolf shook his head. "They're not on the right trajectory."

"That's not what I think they are for that reason," Rayna answered. "It's what a writer called, what I'm guessing were similar lights, when they were being witnessed in the San Luis Valley in Colorado and New Mexico. That was back during the flap of UFO sightings and cattle mutilations that got national attention on the TV show 'Sightings.'"

"This," Trace said waving his hand toward the sky, "has happened before?"

"Something like it has been reported before," Rayna answered. She was careful not to make any assumptions about what they were seeing. As if in reply, there was another flash above their heads. This time, the light traveled in the opposite direction straight across the whole viewable sky and lit up the clouds with an eerie glow.

"It's definitely not lightning. I've never seen anything like it." Rayna stared up at the sky again. "There's been no thunder. The cloud base is pretty low, but these lights are even lower. Plus, these aren't really storm clouds. They're low and dense, but the tops of them are relatively low, too."

"Do you think they're cover for whatever is making the flashes?" Trace asked her.

"I don't know. The flashes are coming from different directions. It's like there's not just one source." Rayna could tell by the look on Trace's face that he wanted a better answer. "Are you asking if I think they are created for the purpose of cover?"

"Exactly!" He answered.

"No, I don't. These clouds are natural. They're a part of a system that we forecasted tonight." Hearing her own voice say those words gave her some comfort. "They are supposed to be here."

"Okay, so what if they are just being used for cover?" Wolf asked.

"It's possible. I think the real question is 'by whom?'"

"Aliens?" Trace asked.

"I hope not," Rayna said as another green flash lit up the night sky.

The three stood in silence watching the sky for more flashes, which came with less frequency until they appeared to stop. It was after midnight when Trace excused himself to go home. Rayna and Wolf bade him goodnight and watched him drive away before Wolf remembered Rayna's tardiness earlier in the evening.

"So, what happened?" He asked her as they walked back toward her truck.

"What happened when?" she asked blankly.

"When you took twice as long to get here than you should have," he answered.

Rayna stopped walking and looked at him. "Twice as long?" She was surprised. "No, I came straight here."

"That should have taken you thirty to forty minutes. It took you over an hour. That's why I texted you."

"Are you sure? I wasn't driving slow, or..." She thought for a moment about stopping on the roadside down the mountain. "Crap!"

"What?"

"I didn't want to tell you about it in front of a stranger."

"What?"

"I saw something, I think, about a half-mile down this road," she answered, pointing to the parking lot exit.

"What did you see?"

"I'm not sure. It was in the shadows. It might not have been anything." Her face lost some color while her mind explored the possible explanations.

"Can you describe what you think you saw?" Wolf put his hand on her right shoulder. His touch gave her some comfort.

Rayna did her best to describe the sense of movement that caused her to stop, trying to use whatever light she could to see what caused it, and staring into the edge of the woods for what she thought had only been a minute or two, at the most.

"I'm sure it was at least an hour before I texted you," Wolf assured her. I was watching the clock. "Did you leave your house right after we talked?"

"Within about 5 minutes. I just stopped to go to the bathroom."

"Then unless you were driving half the posted speed, you were stopped for longer than a minute."

"Ugh! I don't want to think about it." Rayna's mind was racing. She thought of Lee's recovered memories and all of the alien abduction stories she'd read. Ghosts didn't creep her out. Aliens did. "I'm here. I'm fine. I don't want to think about it anymore."

Wolf nodded his head and put both hands on her shoulders and pulled her closer to him to give her a hug. He could tell she was uncomfortable, and he couldn't think of what else to do for her. She turned her head to the side and relaxed it against his shoulder. His arms were strong and warm against the night's growing chill. She took a deep breath and enjoyed the moment. For once, she didn't feel like she was going to faint being so close to him. She felt at ease.

"Should I follow you out of the park?" Wolf asked.

"Are you off duty?" Rayna wondered.

"Not yet, but if it would make you feel better..."

"Thanks, but I'm fine. I just won't be making any unplanned stops between here and my house."

"Probably a good idea. Will you text me when you get home?"

"Yes." Rayna stepped back and looked the ranger in the eyes. "Thank you."

"For what?"

"For worrying about me."

He looked perplexed. "Of course, I worry about you."

Rayna wasn't sure what to say, so she just smiled. He returned the smile, and she turned to walk back to her truck. He walked with her and opened her truck door for her. She climbed in and said, "have a good night, Ranger."

"You, too, Rayna." He watched as she left the parking lot and turned back down the road and away from Bell Mountain.

Chapter 16

Rayna was enjoying a very productive morning forecasting for clients, lining up advertisers and writing proposals when her cell phone rang. The power had come on in the early hours, and the noise of the appliances in the house powering on woke her. She had trouble getting back to sleep so she decided to get an early start. The phone rang again, and she looked at it. She didn't recognize the number, so she didn't answer it. Why ruin her momentum? A minute later, it rang again and showed the same number. This time, she answered. "Hello?"

"Is this Rayna Smith?" The male voice on the other end asked.

"Yes, who's speaking?"

"Ms. Smith, I'd like to ask you a few questions."

"I don't talk to strangers, so you might want to answer mine first. Who is this?"

"A concerned neighbor."

Rayna was becoming irritated. "Without a name, you're a curious stranger."

"My name is… Clint."

"I know most of the people in this town and no one with your name, which makes me doubt you're a neighbor."

"Ms. Smith, I'd like to ask you about your investigation at a certain horse ranch."

"Don't bother. I do not discuss investigations of private residences."

"Oh, really?"

"Really," Rayna said firmly.

"What if I told you that I have information you need?"

"Then I would ask what you could possibly think I need when you just told me that you have questions for me."

"I see," the voice said and paused for a few seconds. Rayna let the silence sink in. "That's too bad," he said, and she heard the phone go dead.

Rayna stared at her phone for a minute. Her mind raced over the possibilities of who Clint might be and if he represented a threat. Realizing that she now had his number, she did an internet search for it, and found nothing. Then, she called the Sheriff's office, and Barb answered the phone, her voice perky as ever.

"Hey, Barb! I need your help."

"What's up?"

"Can you find a way to look up a phone number for me?"

"Why? Did you lose someone's?"

"Nope. I just got a strange call about the Lovell ranch case."

"Oh, sure. Hang on and let me grab a pen, okay?" Rayna heard the sounds of papers rustling and a drawer close on the other end. "Okay, I'm ready."

Rayna rattled off the number and added, "He said his name was Clint and he was a concerned neighbor."

"Neighbor? I don't recognize that area code as anyone around here."

"Neither did I, but with cell phones, that doesn't much matter anymore."

"Right. I'll get on this right away."

"Thanks, dear!"

"I'll call back as soon as I find something," her friend assured her.

"Awesome! Thanks," Rayna said and ended the call.

It was only a minute later when Rayna's phone rang again. "Hello?" Rayna answered.

"Hi, Rayna, I'm glad I caught you," Harold Bender said.

"Hi Harold," Rayna recognized the voice of her forecasting company's very first client. It had a stern quality, but with just a touch of that velvet-like accent of a Southern gentleman.

"Do you have a minute?" he asked.

"I always have a minute for you," she answered.

He cleared his throat, "I know you've had some personal business to attend this week, and you know I don't mind having young Miss Kate fill in for you..."

"Thank you, sir," she interjected.

"You're welcome. However, I thought you might want to know that Kate is attempting to do you a disservice."

Rayna was surprised by his statement. "How so?"

"Well, she asked me if I would follow her if she started a company of her own."

"Really, now?"

"Yesterday. She really tried to turn on that feminine charm, too. She barely stopped short of asking me out for drinks."

"That's beyond inappropriate on so many levels." Rayna felt her face getting hot. "I'm sorry, Harold."

"I was kind of flattered," he continued, "until I realized what she was up to."

"I could fire her for this."

"No need."

"What?" Rayna asked, confused.

"I explained that while she may have the forecasting skills and a pleasant voice, she didn't have the business sense that God gave a brick. Otherwise, she'd understand that what she was doing went against her non-compete clause and betrayed your trust in her."

Rayna loved how loyal Harold was to her, but "thank you," was all she could think to say.

"I just thought you should know. You've been too good to work with to let something like that go without mention."

Rayna smiled. "You are a dear man, Harold, and a great client!"

"She's obviously just a kid," he said in Kate's defense.

"That kid is getting married in a few weeks. She needs a job and a little more maturity. I won't fire her, but I will have something to say to her."

"When will we have the pleasure of your on-air presence again?"

"I'll be back on Monday."

"I look forward to it, then." Rayna could hear the smile in his voice.

"Thank you, again, Harold. Have a great day!"

"You do the same, ma'am."

Rayna hung up the phone and stared at her computer screen for a minute. Damn it! Kate should know better. Rayna wouldn't fire her, but she'd put a little fear in her. There were too many out of work meteorologists out there to risk losing her job by trying to lure away clients from Rayna. What the heck was she thinking?

Rayna's phone rang again, and she made a mental note to change her ring tone. It was getting annoying. She recognized the number as coming from the Sheriff's office. "Hi, Barb," she answered.

"I've got bad news."

"That seems par for the course at the moment," Rayna replied.

"Huh? What's wrong."

"I'll explain later. I guess you couldn't find the number?"

"We did, but it's a scratch phone. There's no name associated with it."

"It figures," Rayna sighed. "Who's we?"

"The cute deputy and I."

Rayna grinned. Barb never missed an opportunity to play the damsel in distress. Rayna knew that Barb could have researched the number herself, but why should she bother when a cute guy was nearby and itching to be close to her? "Nice!" Rayna approved.

"What's going on with you?"

"My only employee hasn't been behaving well. She tried to talk Harold into leaving me and signing up with her."

"Signing up with her?" Barb repeated. "But she works for you."

"Exactly. I guess she wants to go into business for herself by stealing my clients."

"What are you going to do?"

"Well, since Harold asked me not to fire her, I guess I'm going to set her straight and see how she takes it."

"Do you think she'll quit?"

"Not if she's smart, but what she did wasn't very smart, so I don't know."

"Good luck with that! Let me know how it goes."

"Will do. I guess I should get back to work. I've got a few more hours worth yet."

"Me, too." Barb agreed. "I'll talk to you later."

After Rayna finished her work for the day and left Kate a message to come by her house the next morning, she met Sam in town for lunch. It was a pleasant afternoon, worthy of a stroll, so they walked around the little downtown area for a while and discussed who the mystery caller might have been that morning. Sam's curiosity was piqued and he had conspiracy theories on the brain.

"Maybe it was a government agent," he suggested. "Or a man in black."

"Or," Rayna added, "the jerk that broke into my house and didn't find what he was looking for on my drive."

"He'd be pretty bold to call you."

"He was pretty damn bold to break into my house!"

Sam nodded. "True."

"It also could have been someone from another group who caught wind of the investigation and wanted in on it," she thought aloud.

"I doubt that one. There aren't other groups around here – not nearby anyway." He thought for a moment. "No, I think it was someone who wanted to know what you knew but wasn't savvy enough to know how to get you to tell him. That probably rules out MIB."

"Who don't exist." Rayna chided.

"Who you don't think exist." Sam corrected. "We have no good proof either way and too many stories that they do."

"Whatever." Rayna shook her head knowing she'd never win that argument.

"Is that the girl from the horse farm?" Sam pointed down the block at Shana Lovell walking toward them.

"Yes, it is." Rayna smiled at the teenager and waved. Shana seemed happy to see them. As she drew nearer, Rayna asked "What brings you to Jupiter, Shana?"

"Mom had some errands to run, so I tagged along." Shana answered.

"How are things at the farm?" Sam asked in a lowered voice.

"Pretty quiet lately. Unless you count the usual arguments about chores and homework," the girl said honestly.

"You don't do your homework?" Rayna questioned.

"Not as quickly as my parents want me to. I tell them it will be done before it's due. They want it done like within five minutes of my getting home. It's ridiculous." She tossed her head to one side and added, "right?"

Sam nodded, but Rayna didn't show agreement. "I think they just want what's best for you. Does it get done on time?"

"Always, just not on their time."

"I think I'll stay out of this one, then." Rayna smiled. "I don't know much about raising teenagers. I only know how to care for a cat and the big kids around me." She poked Sam in the arm.

Shana laughed. "I don't know. I mean, I like school, but I like hanging out with my friends, too. Sometimes I just need a break."

"I get that," Sam said. "I always wait until just before deadline to write my stories."

"You're probably not helping, Sam." Rayna told him.

"No, but I'm honest."

Rayna turned her attention back to Shana. "So, what's your favorite class?"

"Science!" The girl beamed. "This year we're studying chemistry. It's so easy!"

"Chemistry is easy?" Sam looked confused. "That was my hardest class in high school."

"And that's why you're a reporter, my dear," Rayna told him. "It's good that you like chemistry. We need more girls to be interested in the sciences. The more, the merrier! What makes you like it?"

"I like that it's a fundamental building block type deal and everything has to be balanced. If two atoms go in, then two atoms come out." Shana looked around as if to be sure no one else was listening. "I might even decide to study it in college." She half-whispered.

"Is this a secret?" Rayna asked.

"Sort of," Shana replied. "I don't want my parents to know that I'm thinking about something other than horse farming. They might be unhappy about it."

"Really?" Sam asked. "I'd think they'd be happy no matter what you do as long as your excited about going to college."

"They really want me to run the farm after school, so they can do some traveling. I'd hate to ruin their plans."

"That's very noble of you, Shana, but maybe there's a way you can both have what you want."

"I hope so," the girl said. "I mean, I love horses and that farm, but that's not the life I want."

"What do your friends think?" Sam questioned. "Are they going to college, too?"

"One of them's already in college at Eastern Mountain College. She's taking chemistry and physics there over the summer. She graduated high school last year, and she loves it there. She says it's fun and her chemistry professor is pretty hot. Prof. V she calls him. She's gotten involved with a study group that meets at least once a week." Rayna gave Sam a sly wink. The girl was more talkative than Rayna had seen before and seemed pretty enthusiastic about the idea of going to college. "She said they're going to protest, too."

Sam snapped to attention. "Protest what?"

Shana thought nothing of it. "The power plant. There's a rumor that they've secretly started tritium production again. After the last time, when there was some leakage or something, nobody thinks it's a good idea."

"I doubt they'd start production if they haven't tested for leaks again." Rayna assured her.

"Oh, they'll protest anyway. Do you know what tritium is used for?" Sam played dumb and shook his head, so she answered her own question emphatically, "Bombs!"

"Bombs?" Sam asked.

"Nuclear bombs. That's bad stuff. We shouldn't be making more of those things. We're not at war, right?"

Rayna didn't respond the way she normally would. Instead, she answered matter-of-factly, "I doubt they're making new bombs. Tritium has a short shelf-life and they probably need to replace it in the older, existing bombs."

Shana shrugged. "Either way, bombs are bad."

A voice down the block called Shana's name, and she turned and waved. "Oh, that's Mom. Gotta go!"

"Tell her we said 'hi,'" Sam said as the girl trotted down the sidewalk, which was dotted by the afternoon sun shining through the leaves of the tree-lined town square.

"Will do!" Shana answered over her shoulder.

Rayna stood a little closer to Sam and asked quietly, "Tritium is secretly being made at the nuclear plant? Shouldn't there have been an announcement or hearing or something?"

"Yeah," Sam answered quietly. "That would be some story if the plant were making tritium rods again. I wonder why 'Prof. V.' didn't mention that."

"I wonder if he knew." Rayna thought out loud. "You know... I saw his officemate with a group of students at the buffet the afternoon after I went to get the soil readings from Vincent. I wonder if that's the group she's talking about."

"What was that guy like?"

Rayna remembered the yucky feeling his handshake gave her when she met him and she shuddered. "Nasty energy and a definite jerk. He had some smartass comment about my being a weather girl."

"Oh, he doesn't know you well enough to be a smartass about that." Sam teased.

"No, he doesn't. Don't worry. I didn't let it go unanswered."

"I wouldn't expect you did."

Rayna changed the subject. "Do you still have contacts at the TVA and the DOE?"

"Yes, several." Sam grinned.

"Do you want to give them a call and see what you can find out?"

"I've already made the list in my head. Just gotta get home to the office to find their numbers."

"Good. Let me know what you find. I'm going to call the professor and see if he forgot to mention something important."

Sam hugged Rayna and said, "I'll call you later. Be safe."

"You, too." She replied, and she thought about how lately, after years of just saying it to each other, "be safe" actually had meaning again.

Chapter 17

Rayna's mind was busy trying to make connections that she wasn't even sure were possible as she sat in her office staring at her computer screen. Could the Tennessee Valley Authority be producing tritium rods secretly? If so, with the Lovell farm being downstream from the plant, that might explain the tritium in the soil samples. The problem was that some of those samples were taken quite a ways from the water, which wouldn't make sense if the water was the only source of contamination. Would it? Did all of this somehow tie into the UFO sightings? The dead horse might be explained by lots of tritium contamination, but not the drop from high above the trees. That could not be explained by simple radiation poisoning.

She picked up her cell phone to call Derek and it rang in her hand. She blinked in surprise. It was her sister. "Hi, Dawn!"

"Hey!" Dawn sounded cheerful, but the tone in her voice didn't match the words she spoke. "I have a bone to pick with you!"

"What did I do this time?"

"You neglected to tell me about the hot, new man in your life."

Rayna rolled her eyes. "There's nothing to tell. Who told you anyway?"

"Just because I don't live in your town doesn't mean I don't know people. I can keep an eye on you without even being in the same county!" Rayna knew she was right, but that didn't stop her from trying to keep things private when she knew she'd get crap for them. "Why are you keeping him a secret?"

"I'm not. I just had other things on my mind." Rayna clicked out of the weather model updates and opened up a game of solitaire on her computer. It was her habit to play while on long, drawn out phone calls with family. This call was shaping up to be a bad one already. "Besides, there's nothing to tell. He's just another guy in my life. It's not like I don't already have enough." Of course, Rayna didn't really think Wolf was just another guy, but she'd been down that road before with her sister. It always ended the same. Rayna would be rejected, and her sister would give the useless clichés about there being plenty of fish in the sea and the time not being right or her being too good for the guy. Those words never helped her feel any less hurt, and frankly, she was tired of hearing them.

"You have a lot of guy friends. I'll give you that, but you obviously don't have enough men in your life as far as romance goes. If you're not looking at the ones who practically fall in your lap, you'll never find one!" Dawn offered even more unhelpful advice. She went on for several minutes before Rayna stopped her.

"Do you know how it feels to have that voice of self-doubt in your head convincing you that you will spend your life single and die never having known what it was like to really be loved, to be somebody else's priority? No matter how much I add into my life to fill the void, it's not enough. That loneliness creeps back up over and over."

"Rayna," Dawn tried to interrupt.

"You don't know. Don't even pretend you do. The guys were always lined up waiting for you. Always! Now you're married with three kids. You'll never be alone, and that's great!" She meant it. "I'm happy for you. I just don't know why it hasn't happened for me."

"You're too picky."

"Why shouldn't I be? I know what I want." Rayna's voice cracked with emotion.

"Perfection?" Dawn asked.

"Not at all! I know nobody's perfect. I deserve to have high standards, though. I deserve a smart, funny, decent guy with a job and an understanding of the world. I want someone that I can learn from who's not afraid to learn a thing or two from me, too. He needs to understand and be supportive of my spiritual side, even if he doesn't exactly share it. Most of all he needs to be emotionally available without being obsessive-going-on-psycho. I honestly think those are reasonable requirements!"

"And hot wouldn't hurt," her sister added.

"Right!" Rayna agreed. "Sexy, or it's not going to work, but sexy isn't just about looks. It's about confidence balanced with compassion."

"And you are picky."

"Damn straight I'm picky! I settled for less in the past, and where did it get me? Single again. I'm not going to settle again." Rayna fought the bitterness that crept back up when she thought about the time she wasted on guitar boy. "I spent my twenties waiting on someone who couldn't have cared less about me because he acted like he wanted me when no one else was around to distract him. If it weren't for all the guys who are my friends, I'd really hate men by now. Lucky for me, I don't get along with women very well."

Dawn laughed. "I know. 'Too catty,' right?"

"You know it!." Rayna took a breath. "Why do we have this same conversation over and over when you know what I'm going to say?"

Dawn answered, "Because I always hope you'll have a different answer."

"Me, too."

"Now, tell me about this ranger." Dawn sounded sincerely interested.

"What have you heard?" Rayna never liked to offer more information than she needed to.

"I've heard he looks Indian. I mean like a Native American. He's been spending a lot of time in town, usually with you, and someone told me that you two look like you have some serious chemistry."

"Really? Who said that?"

"I do not divulge my sources." Dawn half-joked.

"I don't know about looking like we have chemistry. We're kind of working a case together, so yeah, he and I are in town together on occasion, but so are Barb and Sam." Rayna kind of liked the idea of mutual chemistry, but in small towns, people exaggerate what they see because it makes the stories more interesting.

"How'd you meet him?"

"I don't know. I guess Barb gets the blame for that. I was on location with the sheriff and Wolf wanted to talk to somebody about some weird stuff happening up on Bell Mountain, where he works. So, she gave him my number."

"Blind date?" Dawn teased her younger sister.

"No! I was pretty mad at Barb when I found out she gave my cell number to a stranger without asking." Normally, Barb would take a witness's number and ask if it was okay to give it to Rayna as a referral, not the other way around.

"Are you still mad?"

"I stopped being mad the minute I saw him." Rayna slipped up. She had just admitted to her sister that the ranger was hot.

"That good looking, huh?" There was a smile in Dawn's tone.

"You know I've always had a thing for Natives. So, yeah, he's pretty hot." Rayna could close her eyes and see his tan skin, dark hair and gorgeous eyes. She decided she might as well tell her sister the rest that only Barb had a clue about. She hadn't really talked to Dawn about a guy openly and honestly since they were teenagers. "In fact, he's so hot that he gives me hot flashes. Literally! When he gets close to me, I think I'm going to have a heat stroke. I can't catch my breath, my face gets hot, and it's all I can do not to fan myself."

"Could be pre-menopause."

"Not funny!" but she heard Dawn giggle anyway. "I'm serious. I've never had a guy affect me like this. I'm not sure I like it. I don't like feeling out of control."

"Do you think it's hormones?"

"I'm not going through menopause!"

Dawn giggled again. "No, I mean do you think you're having some sort of chemical reaction to him?"

"Like pheromones, you mean?"

"Same thing."

"I don't know." Rayna sighed. "I think about him all the time. I love getting to spend time with him, but then he gets close to me and I feel like I'm going to fall down if I don't get away from him. I can't explain it."

"You're in love!" Dawn was almost giddy. "Rayna's in love!" she sang. "Rayna and... what did you say his name is?"

"Wolf."

"Rayna and Wolf sitting in a tree," she chanted.

Rayna rolled her eyes. "Oh, grow up!"

Dawn just laughed. "Come on! It's my job to tease you no matter how old we are."

"Yeah, yeah. I get it. Now you're going to make me sorry I told you."

"No, I'm not."

"And don't tell Mom, please. I don't think I can handle the third degree right now. I've got enough going on."

"Oh? What else is going on?" Dawn sounded suddenly serious.

Rayna realized she had slipped up again. She hadn't told her family about the case, the missing laptop, Lee's disappearance and reappearance, the break-in, or any of the other odd things that had happened in the past few weeks. "Oh, just business as usual." She tried to cover her tracks. "You know. I have a case I can't talk about, a business to run, and research to do."

Dawn didn't think anything of it, thankfully. "Yeah, I guess that could be stressful enough without Mom breathing down your neck or blowing up your phone."

Rayna was relieved. "I need to get back to my afternoon updates. I gave Kate the day off since she'd been helping out more than usual lately."

"Oh, okay."

"I'll talk to you later."

Dawn agreed and said "goodbye."

Rayna hung up the phone and put her head on her desk. Her own thoughts distracted her again. Now she was thinking about Wolf and what his kisses might taste like – that is, if she ever had the chance to kiss him. She really didn't like letting Dawn and Barb talk her into letting herself think a guy like that could be into her. Mutual chemistry? He didn't look like he was going to pass out when she was close to him. Nope, no blushing on his part. He just acted calm, cool, and collected. Of course, she knew that men don't show it the same way, but she still tried to talk herself out of believing there was even a chance with him. As much as she wanted it, it would be too painful when the reality of rejection hit again. The path of her thoughts started winding from warm ones about Wolf to the darker, colder reality of always being the single one.

Solitude is only good when you need it. Rayna rarely needed it. As busy as she kept herself, she stayed calm and grounded most of the time. She had learned at a young age that panicking only wasted time and energy, and nothing was worth panicking over. So, when things got chaotic, she would just take a deep breath and a step back.

Rayna rarely wanted solitude either. She kept herself busy because free time and no one to share it with just reminded her that deep down, she was lonely. No matter how she tried to cling to the clichés about being how happy with yourself was more important than being happy with someone else, she knew better. Loneliness sucks. Sure, she was happy with herself, thankful for her friends and family, and thrilled with the cool experiences she'd had over the years, but when her world got quiet and her projects were complete, she was still alone.

Her sister would never understand. Barb would never try to understand. Sam might, but Rayna doubted it. At that moment, the only person who came to mind that might get it was Jess. Jess – that pathetic, beautiful creature that ended things with Wolf even thought they were probably already over before she made her statement. Of all the people in the world, why was Jess the only other lonely one to come to mind? Probably because Rayna and Jess had two things in common: loneliness and a hot ranger that stayed on both of their minds more than they wanted to admit.

Rayna stared at her phone and wished it would ring. She didn't care who was on the other line. She just needed a distraction, which was all any of her activities ever amounted to – distractions from the reality of loneliness and the fear of spending her whole life single.

The phone didn't ring. Instead, Cloud appeared at Rayna's feet and meowed. Cloud, her favorite counselor, always knew when Rayna needed her. The little black cat jumped up in Rayna's lap and put her front paws on Rayna's chest, sniffed her nose, and then head-butted Rayna on the chin with a loud purr. Rayna didn't need solitude. She just needed a good, furry head-butt to snap her out of the funk she was sliding into.

Rayna's phone alerted her to a text. "Got some news. Can I come over?" It was Sam.

"Yes, please!" Rayna answered and then looked around the office to make sure it was neat enough for company.

"I'll be there in ten." He replied.

Rayna had barely read his text when her phone rang. It was Feildman who also wanted to stop by. Her little house wasn't quite ready for several guests, so she decided it was time for a meeting at the diner. She told the guys she would buy this time, and they agreed it was a good idea.

They arrived at the diner before the dinner rush. Somehow Rayna beat both men there by mere seconds. Sam was full of energy and couldn't wait to get seated and get the meeting started. "Great news!" he said.

"Really? What is it?" Rayna asked.

"I finally got in touch with someone from the TVA!"

He paused for dramatic effect, so Rayna inserted, "and?".

"That's it. I got nothing. In fact, I think I was stonewalled." Fieldman looked disappointed, but Sam wasn't deflated.

"So, nothing, in this case, might mean something?" Rayna hoped out loud.

Sam answered, "that's my thinking. If they weren't producing tritium rods, they would just say it straight up. Instead, I'm getting the run around, which seems to have just ended with a 'no comment' from upper management. Nobody wants to talk, but nobody wants to lie either."

Fieldman smiled weakly. "Okay, so that explains the tritium in the creek bed at the ranch. Now how do we explain the radium on the mountain, the kidnapping of a friend, a break-in at Rayna's, the green lights on Bell Mountain that Rayna and the rangers witnessed, and Rayna's encounter on the side of the road?" Rayna had forgotten she'd told him about that part.

Sam started his deep, boisterous laugh. "One thing at a time, man! That's all I've got!"

Rayna held up her hand. "Let me try, and this is going to sound a bit self-centered, but I can't help it. Somebody wanted the info I've found in my research, so they stole my laptop after freezing it up. Then they broke into my house because what they thought was on my laptop wasn't. The triangle and radium on Bell Mountain were an intricate and intentional misdirect so we'd stop looking for who kidnapped Lee. The green lights were a natural phenomenon that I've never read or heard about *ever*. The encounter on the side of the road was a misidentification or pure imagination altogether. I mean, hell! I wasn't sure I really saw anything to begin with there."

Sam and Fieldman stared at her blankly. Then Sam laughed again. "Bullshit, Rayna! I know you don't believe that!"

Fieldman grinned at her and nodded. "That was quite self-centered, and I don't buy it."

Rayna returned his nod and said nonchalantly, "Occam's Razor."

"No way!" Sam argued. "You can't fall back on that this time because not even that makes sense! There's no simplest explanation for all of it. You left out the UFO that you and Wolf saw. You said yourself that you've never been as freaked out as you were on the side of the road, and remember, you're *fearless*! The lights and that hum aren't natural! They're only reported in UFO cases!"

Fieldman added, "Normally Occam's Razor holds, but Sam's right. Not this time. If the simplest explanation for each item in the list held true, maybe. Unfortunately, too much of this list does not have any logical, acceptable explanation. Then when you put all of the pieces together, even if they are pieces of a couple of different puzzles, the pictures are incomplete and too difficult to explain.

Rayna threw her hands in the air in mock disgust. "I tried. My skeptic friends would be satisfied with my explanations."

"Are you satisfied with them?" Sam asked.

"Not at all. I just needed to try to play devil's, or skeptic's, advocate. You're right. I can't sell myself on Occam's Razor this time. There aren't enough logical, rational, simple explanations for everything that's happened so far."

Fieldman leaned back in the booth and stretched his arms in the air above his head. "So, where does that leave us? What's our next step?"

Sam suggested they check out the caves on Bell Mountain. "I was thinking about it last night. They'd be a good place for a covert operation. The hum reports have mostly been around the mountain. Maybe it's something inside it."

"Those caves are supposed to be closed up now," Fieldman said.

"Yeah, but there are openings all over that mountain. One might have been overlooked." Sam looked at Rayna with a sly grin. "Rayna, want to call your ranger and see if he's willing to give us a tour?"

"He's not *my* ranger!" Rayna protested, but found her cheeks getting warm anyway.

"Yeah," Fieldman played along, "but I'm sure he's willing!" The guys laughed, and Rayna tried not to smile at their boyish jokes.

Chapter 18

A blanket of thin, gray and white clouds stretched from horizon to horizon. There was a light breeze and the air was thick with moisture, but Rayna knew they'd be lucky to get some sprinkles out of this system. "It's okay," she told herself, "Rain will only make the grass grow faster and there's no time to mow the yard." She was on her way to pick up Sam at his house. The pair were going to meet Wolf and Fieldman at Bell Mountain.

There was an area of the park where a cave system cut through the side of the mountain. The entrances had been cordoned off by the rangers, but teenagers still managed to find their way in there to explore, make out, and whatever else they thought they could get away with. If the source of the odd hum was mundane, the group hoped to find it inside the mountain.

Sam's little house reminded Rayna of a mountain top chalet in the Swiss Alps. It was an A-frame made of dark wood with a wide-open living area on the ground level and a bedroom loft at tree level. Rayna had always thought it looked cute, but completely out of place at the edge of their little town in the valley. She was also surprised that Sam bought the place. It never seemed to fit his style, which was more along the lines of the old farmhouses that dotted the area.

Sam, ever the newsman, was waiting for her just inside his front door with journal, pen, and point-and-shoot camera in hand. He rarely went anywhere without those three things. Sure, he might leave them in his car in town, but they were always easily accessible. Luckily, the items were also quite useful for investigating non-newsworthy, paranormal incidents. Sam traveled light, and Rayna always had her go-bag in her truck, which included the same items plus a tape measure, K-2 meter for measuring electromagnetic field fluctuations, a digital voice recorder and extra batteries.

Sam strolled to the truck, opened the passenger door, and grinned at his friend. "Are you ready for this?"

"It ought to be fun!" Rayna answered. "I love hiking. Don't you?"

"You know I do," He got into the pickup and closed the door," but I'm not sure about underground hiking. Those caves might be tight."

"I don't know. I've been in some pretty big caves. It's amazing what kind of wide, open spaces you can find underground."

"I can only hope." Sam grinned again. That smile rarely left his face. Even when he had reason to grimace, he usually hid everything behind that big, wide smile. It was for that reason that people warmed up to him quickly.

Rayna's little pickup navigated the gravel road past the "official use only" sign on the gate that Wolf had unlocked for them. He was to meet the group at the entrance to the caves just beyond the somewhat overgrown parking lot. Rayna marveled at how nature takes back anything left alone for very long. The lot was marked by the same gray gravel stone that was on the rarely used road leading up to it. The wooden beams outlining the area were aged and rotting, and throughout the lot, bits of grass and goldenrod stood tall.

Rayna parked, got out of the truck, and took a deep breath. The air was moist and clean. The voices of dozens of varieties of birds filled her ears. A blue dragonfly flitted past her. "I like this," she said, looking around.

Sam got out of the truck and stretched. "Yeah, it's kind of nice."

The sound of the birds gave way to the crunch of gravel under the wheels of a car entering the lot. It was Fieldman. Right behind his gray sedan was Wolf's Park Service Jeep.

When the group was assembled and ready to go, they found the winding path at the back edge of the lot and trekked into the forest. The hike to the cave entrance was less than a quarter mile, but the path had not been maintained. In fact, the rangers' hope was that it would eventually be reclaimed by the undergrowth in order to thwart the efforts of kids who were out looking for trouble. It took nearly twenty minutes to get to the caves. A sign on the dead-bolted door that had been embedded into the natural passage warned of the dangers of entering. *No trespassing. Danger. Keep out.*

"Is this the only way in?" Sam asked as Wolf thumbed through his keys to find the right one.

"The only one that's easy to get to, yes." He answered, finding the key and jiggling it in the lock.

"There are a few others," Rayna added. "I remember one up a ridge that I found by accident when I was a kid."

"Sure. It was an accident." Fieldman teased her. "We all know what a troublemaker you are."

"You'd have a hard time finding it again," Wolf replied. "The vegetation is all grown up there and a rockslide last winter changed the landscape even more." He finally got the lock to budge and opened the door slowly.

"So there are other ways in that aren't locked up tight?" Sam asked.

"Yes," was Wolf's straight answer.

Rayna and Wolf ventured into the opening of the cave. She looked back at her old friend, still outside the door, and stopped. "Sam," she said quietly, "come on."

"You know, Rayna, I'm not real big on tight, dark spaces."

"It's cooler in here," Wolf offered.

"Really?" Sam questioned.

"About 58 degrees year-round," Rayna answered.

"Besides," Wolf added, "the cave opens up a bit past the entrance. You'll be fine."

Fieldman pushed past Sam. "Come on, big guy. You can handle it."

Sam followed reluctantly. The entry to the cave was narrow with a low ceiling, and Sam had to enter shoulder first and head down. Wolf had been correct, though. About ten feet inside, they found a chamber the size of Rayna's bedroom.

It wasn't long before the light spilling into the cave from the entrance faded into the darkness behind them. Each carried a flashlight, which brightened the floor and walls of the cave just enough to safely pick their way through the increasingly narrow passage. Rayna tried not to look too closely at the walls. Her fear of spiders overtook her in places like this. Sam was dealing with fears of his own. The smaller the space became, the slower the big guy moved. Rayna heard his breathing, heavy and difficult, behind her. "Are you okay, Sam?" she asked.

"Um," he took a labored breath, "not really." The group halted. Rayna turned her flashlight on her friend. He smiled weakly in the beam, "I'm trying…"

"Stop." Rayna told him.

"Stop?" he repeated.

"You don't have to do this. God knows we couldn't easily carry you out of here if you pass out." She cracked a smile and hoped he would, too.

Sam looked ready to argue, but he knew she was right. Claustrophobia, big guys, and tight spaces do not mix well. "I can't do it." He sighed.

Rayna looked at Fieldman, who shrugged. Wolf cleared his throat and Sam sighed again.

"Are you okay heading back on your own?" Rayna asked.

Sam replied, "Yeah, I'll be fine. We haven't really taken any hard turns, yet."

Fieldman flashed his light off and on thoughtfully. "I'll go with him," he finally said.

"You don't have to," Sam assured him.

Fieldman looked up at Sam's sweaty forehead. "Will you be better when we get back outside in the open air?"

"I should be," Sam nodded.

"Then I'll go with you. You know the rules. We use the buddy system. Nobody goes alone. Besides," he added, "we can hike around a bit and see if we can find some other hidden cave openings."

"Good idea!" Rayna approved.

"Yeah," Sam agreed. "We could do that." The two men headed back in the darkness in the direction from which they'd come. Fieldman stopped and turned back to look at Wolf and Rayna. He shined his flashlight's beam in their faces and said, "now you two don't do anything I wouldn't do!"

Wolf scoffed. Rayna forced an embarrassed laugh and replied, "there's nothing you wouldn't do!" With that, the two friends slowly disappeared into the darkness.

Rayna watched them walk until she could barely make out the dim light of their distant flashlights, and then turned to look at Wolf. She felt a flash of heat to her cheeks when she caught him staring down at her in the darkness. She didn't realize he was standing quite so close. "Alone at last," she thought to herself. "What the hell do I do now?" An instant fantasy had her kissing him, but she quickly squelched that bit of reverie and focused on the task at hand.

He broke the silence first and cleared his throat again. "Ahem. Shall we?" He motioned down the narrow, natural hallway with his flashlight.

"Let's" Rayna answered and began walking in front of him.

The passage got narrower before finally opening up into a chamber about the size of Rayna's kitchen. The ceiling extended up nearly twenty feet, and Rayna imagined it would be a great nesting area for bats. Across the space from them and seven feet apart were two openings. Rayna stopped in the middle of the underground room and whispered, "door number one, or door number two?"

"If I remember correctly, the one on the right is a dead end. It only goes back about twenty feet. The Natives used it for storage."

"You sound like a tour guide," Rayna said quietly. "Door number one it is."

The path beyond the opening twisted and turned down a slope into the belly of Bell Mountain. After what seemed to be a quarter of a mile, it leveled out into another chamber. This one was much smaller with stalagmites standing nearly as tall as Rayna. She could hear water dripping from the stalactites above, and she and Wolf paused near the center of the room to take it all in. Pointing her flashlight up toward the ceiling, she admired the natural beauty of the stalactites and silently wondered how old they were. Wolf was shining his flashlight around the space when the beam landed on the opening to the next passage way. He tapped Rayna's shoulder and motioned for her to move in that direction.

"Still no sign of anyone down here," she whispered over her shoulder.

"Not yet," Wolf replied, "but we still have a ways to go."

The pair were about to leave the room when Wolf heard a soft sound behind them. He stopped walking and gently tugged at Rayna's shirt sleeve. Obediently, she stopped and looked at him. Then she looked over his shoulder toward the wide chamber behind them. She'd heard nothing.

Wolf turned back into the chamber but stayed in the natural doorway with Rayna to his right. He swept the flashlight's beam slowly from side to side. Rayna watched the shadows that the light hitting the stalagmites cast on the opposite wall. On his return sweep, something looked out of place. Wolf saw it, too — a shadow whose shape was all wrong.

He pointed the light steadily through that part of the room just to the left of the opening they had entered through. From behind the largest stalagmite, crept a figure. It was low to the ground, crouched, and still partially veiled in shadow. Rayna gasped as the figure straightened himself up into a man of medium height who was facing them with his back to the chamber entrance. To her horror, she realized the light was glinting off a gun in his left hand and it was pointing at her!

Chapter 19

Rayna also realized the man with the gun had a familiar face. "You!" She hissed in disbelief.

"Get that light out of my eyes!" Gregory Hampton barked.

Wolf lowered the light so that it was only shining on the gun. "Who are you?" He asked.

"FBI," Hampton answered.

Rayna looked at Wolf whose eyes were fixed on the gun. She nudged him with her left shoulder. "Isn't this your jurisdiction, Ranger?"

"Yes," Wolf answered without changing his gaze.

"Then why is he pointing a gun at us?" She asked while staring Hampton down. She understood at that moment the nasty energy she felt when he shook her hand in Professor Vincent's office. He wasn't just your average jerk. He was a liar and up to no good.

"Shut up!" Hampton directed.

"Don't quite know," Wolf answered, finally glancing at Rayna to his right.

"Shut up!" Hampton repeated.

"I mean," she continued, "if this is your jurisdiction, we're not doing anything wrong. I'm here with a ranger. I'm not trespassing. So, I'm trying to figure out why some college professor claiming to be FBI is pointing a gun at me."

"At both of you," Hampton corrected. "Don't get smart, Ranger. Hands where I can see them."

"No problem," Wolf answered, and Rayna wondered if he even had his gun on him.

"I see a problem," she said.

"Shut her up!" Hampton demanded.

"You're the one with the gun, and she's not listening to you. What makes you think I can shut her up?" Wolf looked at her and smirked.

Rayna's eyes darted from Hampton's face to something behind him and back. Hampton and Wolf both saw the motion. Then she did it again – a glance from him to behind him. "If you're really FBI, show us your badge," she finally said defiantly while focusing on Hampton briefly, and then glancing at Wolf. Wolf caught her glance and saw her eyes dart back to the space behind Hampton. Wolf's eyes followed. Hampton caught their movements. He was getting nervous.

"Later." Hampton said. "Now be quiet and listen…" He couldn't take it anymore. In the split second that he turned his head around to stare into the nothingness behind him, Rayna turned to push Wolf down the dark passage to his left. Simultaneously, Wolf grabbed Rayna's left arm and pulled her behind him. Then came a flash and a loud bang accompanied by searing pain in Rayna's right arm.

There wasn't time to think. They ran down the corridor as quickly as they could, ducking to the next turn off on the right, and then the one behind that on the left. Rayna tried to look behind them to see if Hampton was following, but with the only flashlight in Wolf's hand pointing in front of them, she saw nothing but darkness. Her mind raced with a million thoughts. "Keep running! Where's my flashlight? Why the hell was a science teacher just shooting at us? Why does my arm hurt?" As they rounded a bend the flashlight beam gave way to a brighter light. "Thank God! There's a way out!" Rayna said aloud.

"Um… yeah," Wolf said. He stopped suddenly at the opening and held his hand behind him to slow her. "Maybe not what you had in mind."

"Shit!" Rayna stared at the river flowing about 25 feet below the cave opening and the sheer drop that lead to the fast-moving water.

"Gun or river?" Wolf asked.

Rayna didn't have to think. "River."

Wolf jumped first and was quickly taken downstream by the current. Rayna closed her eyes and took a leap of faith. The mountain water was frigid. Rayna's arm throbbed. The current was swift. "Now what?" Rayna thought.

It wasn't long before the cave exit was out of site. Wolf and Rayna struggled against the river current to get to the bank. Rayna wasn't the strongest swimmer and the pain in her arm wasn't making it any easier. Wolf was about fifty feet ahead of her yelling something. Rayna couldn't make out his words but guessed his meaning when she saw the fallen tree, half on land, half in the water ahead of them.

Wolf got to it first. The current was rougher there as the water pushed its way around and under the obstacle. Still, the tree gave him something to hold onto as he made his way along side it to the shore line. He paused to watch Rayna slam into it. She let out a little shriek of pain, and her head went under the water's surface.

"Shit!" Wolf said and left the shore to swim to her. Then her head popped back up. Rayna was trying to get a grip on the tree with her left hand. "Use both hands!" Wolf yelled over the sound of the rushing river.

"I can't!" Rayna yelled back.

Wolf edged along the giant trunk, grabbed her left arm, and in one swift move, threw it around his neck as he turned back toward the bank. Rayna was grateful for the help, but still struggling to keep a hold of him without strangling him.

Exhausted, they crawled out of the river onto the bank. Wolf was basically carrying her on his back. When they were clear of the water, she slid down and sat on the grass beside him trying to catch her breath. "Ow," she moaned quietly when the adrenaline subsided and the pain in her arm returned with a vengeance. She looked at her right sleeve. It was covered in blood. She realized the throbbing was coming from the back of her arm, and it was too painful to twist it around to try to look at it.

Wolf saw red streaked down the right side of Rayna's soaked shirt. "What happened?" He moved around behind her to get a better look.

"I think that jackass shot me."

"This is gonna hurt."

"It already does."

Wolf pulled Rayna's sleeve away from the wound. She winced in pain. "I've got good news and bad news," he said.

"Good news first," Rayna said through clenched teeth.

"There's not a bullet hole, but you're missing some flesh. I think it grazed you. Do you want the bad news?"

"'You're missing some flesh' wasn't the bad news?"

"No. The bad news is that Barb will never be able to tease you about wearing this ugly, flowered shirt again." He took his multi-tool from his belt and cute the sleeve off Rayna's shirt.

"How did you know she teased me about it?"

"She's your best friend, and this doesn't seem to be your style. I figured she teased you mercilessly at some point."

"You figured right. It's not my style and she scolded me for trying something new because I'm never supposed to experiment with fashion without her input." Rayna sighed. "You might as well cut the other one off, too. I hate asymmetrical styles." She joked.

Wolf agreed, and cut the other sleeve off, too. In the absence of a clean cloth, he used it to apply pressure to the wound.

"You've been wanting to do that all day, haven't you?" she asked.

"What?"

"Trim this garden," she answered pointing at the floral print. Wolf laughed and shook his head. "Oh, and remind me to never go into the make-out caves with you again!" she added.

He chuckled and then got serious again. "We need to keep pressure on this for a while and see if it stops bleeding before we do anything else. How are you feeling?"

"Is that a trick question? It hurts like hell."

"I'm being serious. You're not light-headed or anything, are you?"

"No, but I hate medical stuff. I'm trying not to think about it. I nearly pass out when I have to have blood drawn." All the times that she'd had to lie down after being pricked by a needle when she was a child rushed back to her memory. "Yeah. I really need to not think about it."

Wolf moved from behind her to beside her, so he could hold the fabric to her wound but see her face while they talked. "Try to hold your arm up a little higher, okay." She lifted her elbow in response. "Good." He paused. "So, what do you want to talk about?"

"Anything," she answered, staring at the ground in front of her. He was silent for a moment, and she decided to be brave and ask him something that truly could provide a distraction. "Do you mind if I ask a personal question?"

"Probably not," he answered.

"Why aren't you married?" There. She had asked it, and she expected an uncomfortable pause as soon as the words left her mouth. He surprised her by answering as if he'd been thinking about it himself.

"Until recently, I never thought marriage was my path."

The words sounded strange to Rayna's ears. She turned her head to look him in the eyes. "What changed?"

"Sometimes you meet someone, and that person brings you to a crossroads and forces you to rethink your path." He smiled, weakly at her. "Why aren't you married?"

"I was once, briefly. That turned out to be more of a detour than a path." She thought about guitar boy, as she and Barb called him. He loved those instruments more than anything, including her.

"Really?" He asked. "What happened?"

"Apparently, he realized that he took a wrong turn."

"I'm sorry."

"Don't be," she told him. "I'm better off without him. I just chalk it up to a learning experience."

"What did you learn?"

Rayna looked back down at the ground in front of her again. "That I deserve a man who wants to be with me because he loves me and not because everyone tells him he should be with me."

"Would you do it again?"

Rayna scoffed. "Marry him? Hell no!"

Wolf shook his head, and the movement made her look directly at him again. "No, I mean get married, in general."

She smiled. "I'd like to. I would like to think that there is somebody for me, and that I'll meet him in this lifetime."

"What if you already have?" He dropped his gaze to where he was holding the fabric to her wound.

"Then he needs to make himself known. Life can be too short… too short to waste time. It's a cliché, but true."

His eyes dropped farther to the ground behind her. "No doubt," he said quietly.

The hike back to the parking lot was long, uphill, and bumpy. Wolf and Rayna made their own trail. He knew which direction to take and led the way. Rayna did the best she could to hold her arm up and walk behind him, occasionally using the uninjured left arm for balance. Her blue jeans and shirt started to dry along the way, but her shoes were so waterlogged that they felt like they weighed an extra ten pounds. She hated wet shoes. Wolf seemed to be handling everything okay. His pace was slow, and he kept looking behind him to check on her. "Still here," she'd say with a half-hearted grin, trying to hide how miserable her arm was making her. For an area so small, missing a chunk of it sure hurt like hell.

Sam and Fieldman were leaning against Rayna's pickup chatting when she and Wolf broke through the brush on the lower side of the parking area. Their noise caught the other investigators' attention, and the look of Rayna with her blood-stained shirt and her arm held up in the air made Sam stop cold. "What the hell?" he asked. "Are you okay?"

"Uh-huh," Rayna nodded.

"No, really! Are you okay?" He walked toward her as fast as he could.

"Yes," she answered, more determined to be convincing. "Why do you ask?"

"Your shirt is covered in blood. What the hell happened to your arm?" Sam was clearly concerned but fought the urge to touch her.

"She was shot," Wolf answered for her.

"Shot at. *We* were shot at," Rayna corrected him. Then she thought for a second and got mad again. "That jerk shot at me!" she yelled.

Both men looked accusingly at Wolf.

Wolf raised both hands in the air. "Not me! The other jerk!"

Rayna giggled quietly. "Wolf saved me, sort of."

"Clearly," Fieldman said calmly, "you weren't just shot at. You were hit."

"I'm okay. The bullet just grazed me."

"You think?" Sam walked to her side to examine her arm.

"You know how I hate blood?" she asked. "I'm trying not to think about it."

Sam told her, "you need to go to the hospital."

"She's going, but she insisted on finding you two first, and our vehicles were here anyway." Wolf pointed toward their cars.

"You look pretty pale," Fieldman observed.

"Thinking about it gets me woozy," Rayna answered, and started walking toward her truck.

"I meant Sam," Fieldman said.

Sam's voice was shaky. "She got shot! It could have been worse."

"It's okay," Rayna assured him. "Let's just go. I think my keys are still in my right pocket, but I can't get them with my left hand." She thrust her hip toward Sam. "Can you grab them? I don't think I should drive."

Sam nodded and gently reached into her tight front pocket to pull out her keychain. "Why are your pants damp?"

"It's a long story."

As the reality settled in, Sam had more questions, which came in rapid fire while they walked to the truck. "Who shot you? Why did someone shoot you? Did Wolf shoot them back? Oh, God! There's not a dead body in the caves somewhere, is there? Or did you get shot in the caves? Where the hell were you just coming from? That's not the direction of the entrance we used."

"It's a long story." Rayna repeated. "I'll tell you on the way." She looked back at Wolf. "Can you call Barb for me, Wolf, and tell her what happened?"

"Yes, ma'am! Want me to call a family member, too?"

"Hell no!" Rayna flinched at the thought of her mother or sister finding out about this. No, they could wait. Barb needed to know and would find out fast anyway.

"Fieldman," Sam called. "Are you coming?"

"I'll meet you there." Fieldman got into his car and waved.

Then Sam asked, "Ranger, are you coming?"

"No. You can handle this. I've got a guy with a gun on park property who's already shot one person. I need to call for help and find him."

"Yeah, I guess you do," Sam said as he opened the passenger side door for Rayna. "Now, Darlin', why are you wet?"

103

Chapter 20

Jupiter might have been the county seat and the biggest town in the county, but that wasn't saying much. What passed as a clinic in a larger city was "the hospital" in Jupiter. It was large enough to have an emergency room and one operating room for those people who couldn't wait to travel to a bigger town a county or two away. There was a helicopter pad on the roof for those rare instances that emergency transport needed to be faster than an ambulance could go on windy mountain roads.

Other than farming or automobile accidents, not many emergencies happened in Jupiter that required advanced care. It was just a quiet town with two diners, an ice cream shop that was only open in the summertime, a few county buildings, a Sheriff's Office, and a school that housed kindergarten through twelfth grades. All of that, and it had a clinic with just enough staff to take care of whatever might happen in a small town, which did not normally include a meteorologist getting mysteriously shot in her tricep while out on a hike on Bell Mountain.

The place was buzzing, and Rayna knew it was only a matter of time before someone who was randomly connected to her sister was making that dreaded phone call. Of course, a call like that would violate all sorts of policies, both local and federal, but that wouldn't stop someone from leaking information to Dawn. She was worse than the press or the FBI. She had ears everywhere.

Rayna hated the sling the nurse gave her. It was tan and boring. It also didn't help that the thing would draw attention to her unusual injury. She wanted to keep what happened as quiet as possible. How she could do that was a mystery though. Even if nobody called Dawn, her best friend was a reporter, the whole town knew her, and the Sheriff's office had her number on speed dial, or at least

Barb did. Yep! There was not getting around it. That call from her sister, her mother, or her grandmother was going to come. How was she going to explain this one?

She left the emergency room area of the little county hospital in a grumpy mood. Sam and Fieldman walked silently on either side of her down the stark white hallway toward the main lobby. Neither could think of anything cheerful to say. As they rounded a corner, they found a tall, broad-shouldered man in a dark suit standing in the center of an otherwise empty hall facing them. He had a look of expectance on his face.

"Rayna Smith?" he asked.

"Yes," she answered.

"I need you to come with me," he said as his hand reached toward her good arm.

Rayna stepped back. Sam and Fieldman reflexively stepped in front of her as a unified shield.

"Who are you?" Sam asked, puffing up like an angry bear.

"Federal Agent Trent Black," he answered and reached into his back pants pocket to pull out his wallet. "I'm with the FBI." He flipped the wallet open and showed them what looked like a legitimate badge to Rayna.

Sam laughed. "For real? That name sounds like something straight out of a movie. Is that the best you've got?"

The agent did not laugh. "Most people think it's funny. My parents did not."

Fieldman finally spoke up, "What does the FBI want with our Rayna?"

"We just want to talk with her," Agent Black answered.

"About what?" Rayna asked.

The agent pointed at her right arm hanging in its boring tan sling. "Your new accessory."

"Was that a joke?" Sam scoffed. "Mr. My Parents Didn't Think It Was Funny made a joke?" His voice echoed down the hallway. The agent did not lift his gaze from Rayna.

"Ma'am, will you please come with me? My partner is waiting."

"We're coming, too," Fieldman announced.

The agent shook his head. "You're not invited."

"I'm Rayna's ride home. She needs me," Sam assured him.

"I'm sure we can accommodate her," the man in the black suit answered.

Rayna stepped out from behind her friends. "It's okay, guys. Let me just get this over with. I have a few questions for him myself. If this is the last you see of me, tell the world that Agent Black, the aptly named MIB got me." Sam gave a weak grin, and Fieldman's face was turning red with anger. Rayna turned to follow the agent down the corridor to the exit and paused to call behind her, "Sam, tell Barb and Wolf to meet me at Pat's Diner at 8:00."

"Pat's?" Sam repeated.

"Yes, Pat's!" With that, Rayna exited the building and followed Agent Black to a gray, unmarked, mid-sized sport utility vehicle, where his smaller, younger coworker waited in the driver's seat. He gave Rayna a nod as Agent Black opened the back door and motioned for her to get into the car.

Rayna watched the little hospital, or big clinic depending on her mood, shrink into the background. She could make out her friends standing outside the main entrance watching the SUV she was inside driving down the road to the main street through Jupiter. Her arm was throbbing. She never realized how much she used her right tricep until she felt searing pain every time she forgot that she wasn't supposed to move it. That boring beige sling was beginning to make more sense, even if she just used it to remind herself to keep that arm still. She had always had a high tolerance for pain medication, and she couldn't remember if she had explained that fact to the emergency room doctor, who seemed to have been in a hurry to treat her and send her on her way.

It wouldn't be long before the whole town heard about what happened. Unfortunately, very little of what they heard would be accurate. Word spreads like wild fire when it involves a mystery or a scandal. The town's most famous resident, which wasn't saying much, was just treated for a gunshot wound after being driven back from somewhere out of town. Then after being quickly stitched up, she was escorted out of the hospital by a strange man in a black suit driving a dark, unmarked vehicle. Surely people would have noticed. Hopefully, they noticed, and maybe someone got the license plates on that dark vehicle. Maybe that's what Sam and Fieldman were doing outside the hospital entrance, or maybe they were berating each other for not insisting on accompanying her.

Rayna suddenly felt more vulnerable than she remembered feeling her whole life. The stories she had read about the men in black rushed to her mind: threats to keep quiet, questionable behavior from supposed government agents, a distaste for assertion of your rights, suspicious deaths of witnesses... "Crap!" she thought. "What the hell have I gotten myself into now? What if that ID badge was a cover? Why didn't I insist someone come with me instead of saying I'd be okay? Where the hell are they taking me?"

Rayna knew they weren't driving to the county buildings. Instead, she realized they were driving toward the lonelier edge of town. She took a deep breath and tried to calm her racing mind. She decided she needed to focus on their surroundings in case she needed to run. Now there was a fun thought!

The car ride only took five minutes. The men brought Rayna to an office park not far from the medical center and farther from the center of Jupiter. Half of the buildings appeared empty, their windows dark and staring down at the SUV as it passed. They drove to the building farthest from the main road. It was two stories high, brown brick with cream colored trim, and as bland as the sling on her arm. There were no business names on the sign in front, nor the sign on the door. Except for the light in one downstairs office window, there were no signs of life here either. Rayna guessed that office was where she was being taken, and she was right.

Inside there were two desks void of anything but task lamps. They looked pretty new and sterile. On the back wall, there was a counter with a coffee maker and some Styrofoam cups. It was obvious to Rayna that this office was brand new and probably a very temporary location for these agents.

Agent Black motioned to Rayna to have a seat at one of the desks. "Please," he said, "make yourself comfortable." Nothing about the situation felt comfortable, but she obligingly sat down and watched Black's partner make a small pot of coffee.

"Why am I here?" Rayna gestured to the room around her. "Wouldn't the Sheriff's Office be more useful?"

"Too many people there know you," Black answered. "There wouldn't be any privacy."

"And why do we need privacy?" she tried to keep her voice steady despite her nerves.

"Ms. Smith, can you describe the man who shot you? Did you recognize him?" Black's partner asked her from his stance beside the coffee maker. Rayna noticed the blatant disregard of her own question.

"Can I have your name?" she answered a question with a question. Doing so was a pet peeve, but so was having a conversation before being introduced.

"I'm sorry, ma'am. I'm Agent Neusom Holmes."

"Man!" she thought. "What is with these names?"

Agent Black repeated his partner's question. "Did you recognize the man who shot you?"

"Yes, I did, but I'd guess the name I was told was his was not his real name."

Agent Holmes studied her face. "Why do you think that?"

"College professors don't typically hide in caves and shoot at unarmed people for no apparent reason."

Agent Black sat down in the chair at the opposite desk. "No apparent reason?"

Rayna leaned on the desk. "He was acting like a cornered animal," she said through her teeth. "Suddenly, he was just there with a gun."

Agent Black mirrored her motion. "You weren't looking for him?"

"No." She leaned back into her chair.

Agent Holmes poured himself a cup of coffee. "What were you looking for?"

"Huh?" Rayna didn't have a ready answer.

The younger agent walked over to stand beside Black. "In the caves, what were you looking for?" He asked again. "You and the ranger went in there for a reason, didn't you?"

"How did you know he was with me?" Rayna wondered what else they knew.

Agent Black asked her, "was anyone else with you?"

Rayna paused. She hated lying, and as far as she could tell, they might know the truth anyway. Still, if they didn't know that Sam and Fieldman were there, too, she wasn't going to offer her friends up that way. "It was just Wolf and me," which wasn't totally a lie since they were the only two in the caves when the jerk of a pseudo-professor shot her. "We were looking for the source of the mysterious sound that's been heard and reported all over the mountain."

"Did you find it?" Black asked.

"No, we weren't in there very long before that guy showed up. Do you know what it is?"

"What what is?" Holmes stared into his cup.

"That sound." Rayna answered.

Agent Black answered, "I have no idea what you're talking about," and Rayna believed he was sincere.

The conversation wasn't very helpful to the agents or Rayna. She was guarded in what she told them about the investigation. They were equally guarded in what they told her regarding the man who shot her. His first name was Greg, but his last name was a fake. He had worked for the FBI, and was undercover, but stopped reporting on his progress and had dropped off the radar in the last few days. They knew when the call went out about a shooting in the caves on Bell Mountain that he was likely involved since that was one of the locations he had in his reports.

"What was he investigating?" Rayna asked several times before Agent Black finally half-answered. "A student group."

"A student group," she repeated quietly. Her mind finally started making connections to conversations past. "So, what was he doing in the caves?"

Agent Holmes spoke before Black had the chance to open his mouth. "That's what we'd like to know."

Rayna stood and adjusted her sling for effect. "Well, agents, I'm tired. My arm hurts, and my friends are probably wondering just where on earth you've taken me. They're expecting me at eight o'clock and I'd like to be dropped off at my house by 7:45, please." She knew how to take control of a conversation and get her way. She didn't do it often, but it worked when she did.

"I'm not sure that we're done here," Agent Black said, standing up and towering over her even from across two desks.

She didn't back down. In her mind she was picturing the color yellow and painting her world in it. She took a deep breath and let it out. Then, she stared Agent Black in the eye. "Yes, we are done here, and I need a ride home right now," she stated in a calm, steady, confident voice.

Holmes looked at his taller counterpart whose face softened. "Sir?" he asked.

"Yes," Black nodded, "we're done. We'll take you home."

"But," Agent Holmes started.

"No," Black waved his hand. "We're done."

Chapter 21

Pat's wasn't the good diner, or even the other diner. Pat's was the only place in Jupiter that Rayna knew her little group could have some privacy to discuss the day's events and figure out where to go from there. Pat Monahue was the lunch lady in the cafeteria when Sam and Rayna attended Jupiter Public School. She was middle-aged, with red and gray streaked hair, a thick southern drawl, and a voice like gravel, but she had a heart of gold and the students loved her. So, they nicknamed the lunch room Pat's Place.

Rayna hadn't referred to Pat's since college, but Sam knew exactly what she meant when she suggested meeting there before she left the hospital. Barb had access to the key since it was a county building, the whole place was empty during the summer, and they could park behind the school where no one would see their vehicles. Pat's was the perfect place for a round-table discussion with no interruptions.

Of course, the discussion wasn't going as Rayna hoped so far. She wanted to talk about where to go from there with the investigation. All anyone else seemed to be interested in was her arm, and that was the one thing she was trying her hardest not to focus on. "If one more person asks me 'how are you?' I'm going to lose it!" She warned.

Wolf had just made that little error in conversation starting when he arrived. "Um… okay…"

"She's not good," Sam suggested to him.

"I'm fine." Rayna corrected him.

"Right. She's not good, she's fine." Sam winked at Barb and Wolf sitting across the table from him.

"Look. I got shot in the arm, not the head. My brain still works, my ears still work, my eyes work, and my mouth works." She assured them.

"Boy, does it!" Sam laughed.

Wolf pointed to her sling and said, "your right arm isn't working."

Barb pointed at it, too. "Aren't you right handed?"

"Yes, but I'm…"

"Fine!" Wolf and Sam said in unison. "We get it," Sam added.

Rayna rolled her eyes at him. "Good! Can we just get on with this?"

The door to the cafeteria opened and Fieldman entered. He strode over, took a seat at the end of the table, and looked at Rayna. Then he asked the inevitable, "how are you?"

Rayna put her head on the table with a muffled thud and pretended to bang it a few more times for good measure.

"Not good, huh?" Fieldman asked stone-faced.

Rayna lifted her head to start to speak and Sam answered for her, "she's fine."

"Thanks, Sam," she nodded at him and sat straight up in her chair again. The four friends looked at Rayna expectantly. She couldn't take it. She was tired of wearing her brave face and her big girl panties. She let it go. "Okay, fine! I'm not fine! Some jackass with a gun claiming to be FBI who just last week was only a two-bit jerk of a professor at a local college pointed a gun at me and actually shot at me. He really freakin' shot at me! What the hell did I do? I thought I was chasing strange sounds and lights in the sky, and maybe aliens, but it was a damn *human* that shot me! I'll admit it. I'm a little freaked out! Then, I have to deal with getting stitched up, and then two real federal agents dressed in black like something out of an X-files episode take me to a secluded place to ask me questions about the jerk who shot me because they don't know where to find him! *Nobody* knows where to find him! I'm having a hard time feeling secure in my situation right now. Someone stole my laptop and kidnapped Lee. Someone broke into my house for God knows what, and now someone shot at me, but I don't even know if it's all the same someone! So, you're right! I'm not fine! I'm freaked out and pissed off!" She took a breath and felt her face flushed with anger and embarrassment.

Her four friends just stared at her in silence for a moment. Then, Sam started laughing. It was a big, hearty laugh. "Well, it's about time you started acting like the human that you are!"

Barb reached across the table and patted Rayna's left hand. "It's okay, honey, we're all here for you."

Wolf nodded in agreement. "Sam's right. You're only human. Barb's right. We're right here. We're not going to let anything else happen to you."

Rayna sighed. "I know you'll try. I trust all of you. I just don't know what's next. I mean, how did a hum and a horse being dropped from the sky turn into all of this..." she gestured widely with her left hand, "this mess? At least I know what to expect when we're investigating something mundane like ghosts."

Wolf cleared his throat. "Ghosts are mundane?"

"In my world, yes" she answered. "I know how to protect myself from angry ghosts, which are rare, and other negative entities, which are rarer. I have no clue how to protect myself from aliens, and I obviously never expected to have to protect myself from a person with a gun."

"You handled yourself pretty well, by the way," Wolf flashed an approving grin at her. "You did some quick thinking for someone who'd never been in that situation before."

"What did she do?" Sam asked. He had never gotten the whole story out of Rayna on their way to the hospital. She went from gun to river pretty fast on the way to the hospital.

Wolf shook his head. "She bought us time like a pro."

"Thanks," Rayna interrupted. "Can we just get on with the issue at hand?"

"Which is?" Fieldman asked.

"Which is where are we in this investigation and where do we go from here?" Rayna sat back in the hard plastic, county issued, public school cafeteria chair. "I'm not at Pat's Place for nothing. We need to put everything on the table and try to place the pieces together now, while no one's watching or listening."

Sam asked the first question, at least chronologically, it was the first question. "So, what would be dropping horses from high up over the tree tops?"

"One horse," Fieldman corrected. "What or who, and why?"

Rayna looked at the dirty fingernails on her left hand. "I don't know. We could probably rule out PETA." After a long pause, she added, "On that hard drive, I had saved some articles that I had quickly skimmed over the night before Lee disappeared. They were about these cattle mutilations back in the 1990's in the San Luis Valley of New Mexico and Colorado. A lot of people blamed aliens, but some hypothesized that it was actually the government."

"Of course!" Wolf scoffed. "If you can't blame little green men, blame the men in black."

"I guess," Fieldman said.

"Actually, the blame was on government scientists." Rayna added.

"Why would the government mutilate cattle?" Sam asked.

Rayna explained. "The conspiracy theorists claimed that the scientists were checking for unusually high levels of radiation in the animals' blood and soft tissue. It's the old 'you are what you eat' philosophy. They were either concerned about water or the food supply or something. I didn't finish the articles. I planned to go back to them later, but the drive was stolen."

"What else was on that drive?" Wolf asked.

"More stuff like that. Some old UFO reports that were kind of similar to what we witnessed coming back from Bell Mountain that first night, and I had gone off on a tangent in my research. There were some files about the nuclear facilities around here. The San Luis stories made me curious."

"Files, huh?" Sam leaned on the table.

"Details about how reactors work, byproducts of the process, and disposal issues... lots of stuff." Rayna explained.

"You didn't hack some DOE system, did you?" Sam seemed almost serious.

Rayna threw her one good arm in the air in the universal sign for "I'm innocent" and laughed. "Like I'd even know how! No, I was looking at publicly available information buried deep in websites that very few would think to look at."

Sam smiled. "Always resourceful! That's our Rayna!"

"Did you draw any conclusions?" Fieldman asked.

"No, but I see enough similarities to make me wonder if someone mutilated that horse for research or testing for radiation poisoning." Rayna hated the thought that anyone could be that cold-blooded and twisted as to destroy a horse, which was basically a family pet, just to see if it might eventually get sick.

"But the animals didn't look or act sick, right?" Wolf asked.

Rayna shook her head. "Not while we were at the farm, but they told us that three had been sick the month prior, and one had died. It was an older one, though," she added.

Fieldman observed, "so maybe three sick horses in one month were enough to tip someone off to a potential problem."

"Who else would know about that other than the Lovells and their vet?" Sam asked.

Rayna thought for a moment. "Anyone they mentioned it to, and anyone their 15-year-old daughter might have spoken to. You know how teen girls will talk about anything and everything, especially if there's drama involved."

Rayna saw a look of recognition in Sam's eyes. The proverbial light bulb had gone on over his head. "I bet she mentioned it to one of her friends in that fake professor's class. I bet he was the one leading the student group that was supposedly going to protest the creation of tritium rods." He snapped his finger. "That's it! That's how it ties together!"

"I see," said Barb. She'd been so silent, that Rayna forgot she was sitting there. "So, the horses get sick, and Shana tells somebody. It gets back to pseudo-prof and then to someone in the government who wants to know what's making the horses sick. So, they pick one up, kill it, mutilate it, and drop it from the treetops back on the farm where they stole it from." She nodded approval toward Sam. "Of course, dropping it was a little more dramatic than necessary."

"But that only gives us a small part of this story." Wolf said. "I mean, that's pretty important to your original case, but it doesn't explain the mystery hum on Bell Mountain or the UFOs and green flashes. What did you call them, Rayna? Cheap fireworks?"

"Yeah. Cheap fireworks," Rayna confirmed. "Now that I think about it, those things were seen in the San Luis Valley during the mutilation and UFO flap, too. Actually, the guy who wrote the book about it, coined the term 'cheap fireworks.'"

"So, this is all coming back to the animals on the Lovell farm getting sick." Fieldman didn't look totally convinced.

"Maybe not all of it, but a lot of it," Rayna suggested. "Derek found tritium in the soil on the farm, and the last time that reactor up at Watts Bar made tritium rods, there was a leak and they had to shut it down."

"Right," Sam recalled. "So, if all that stonewalling I got when I tried to follow up with the Tennessee Valley Authority and the Department of Energy meant something, maybe it was that they're producing tritium again, secretly, like Shana rumored, and it's leaking again."

"It would take an awful lot of tritium to kill a horse." Rayna said.

"Yeah," Barb agreed, "but it only killed one, older horse. The other two survived."

Fieldman nodded. "I'm still not sure that explains the ranger's hum, or the UFO's or the triangular burn marks and radiation on Bell Mountain where Lee's car was found."

"No," Wolf concluded. "Something is still missing, but I think we've got a hypothesis to start with."

"Right!" Fieldman agreed. "Let's go with the mundane explanation first and see how far it takes us. Then we'll see if we can figure out the anomalous items later." Rayna was happy that he was willing to start with the easier explanation but noted that he was right. The rest of it would be harder to explain, and they had to try. After all, he was a MUFON investigator.

"Okay," Rayna took the lead, "Sam, can you keep digging a bit more into the DOE and TVA? See if anyone will talk to you off the record or point you in some direction where we can confirm it for ourselves. Barb, please keep your ears open for any sign of a break in my case and Lee's. Knowing that the Sheriff knows us, I'm assuming the cases are still active and they're looking for leads. Am I right?"

"Definitely!" Barb answered.

"Wolf, just do whatever it is you do and keep us posted." He smiled at her when she spoke to him, and her heart raced a little. It was good to know the pain meds didn't numb those nerves either. What was she saying? Oh, yeah. "Fieldman, if you can come up with any leads on the UFOs and green flashes that might narrow that part down a bit, I'd appreciate it. Whatever connections you have, no matter how far-fetched, we need something to go on there."

"I've got some old friends in the military, air force actually, I can call. Not sure where they're stationed now, but I'll start prying a little harder there." He drummed the table, "And what are you going to do, my dear?"

"I'm going to keep researching, and hope nobody else decides I need to be messed with."

"Just hope?" Wolf asked.

"What else can I do?" Rayna said, exasperated.

"Someone needs to keep an eye on you," Sam said.

"No," Rayna answered.

"We can take turns," Barb suggested.

"I'm not on duty again until tomorrow," Wolf said. "I'll take first watch, and I'll start by walking you to your car."

Rayna shrugged. "My truck's at Sam's house. I haven't had a chance to retrieve it, and I don't like driving one-handed."

"Then I'll walk you to your house. It's not far, right?"

"Just a few blocks," she answered. "You don't have to."

Sam pretended to smack the back of her head. She felt the breeze of his hand as it passed by. "Rayna, just take the offer."

"Um… I mean… okay. Thank you." She nodded at Wolf, who smiled at her again. "Yeah," she thought silently, "twist my arm to make me spend time with the hottest guy I know."

The group said their goodbyes and headed for the door. Barb and Rayna held back to turn off the lights and close up the cafeteria so that no one would suspect anyone had been there. "I've got to get a few things from my truck," Wolf said to Rayna. "I'll meet you outside." He left the two women to themselves.

Barb gave Rayna a gleeful smile as soon as the door shut behind him. "Ooh!" she could barely contain her excitement. "He's going to walk you home! How romantic!"

"Shut up," Rayna tried to hide her grin. "It's nothing."

"No, it's something! He volunteered 'first watch.' He cares enough to make sure you'll be alright tonight. Wait! Does that mean he's spending the night?"

"I wasn't planning on an overnight guest." The thought made Rayna extremely nervous. "He's just going to make sure I get home alright. Right?"

"Um, sure."

"Look. I'm in no shape for entertaining. I just want to take some more pain-killers – the ones the doc said only to take if I plan on sleeping – and go to bed." She saw the smirk on Barb's face. "Alone!" she added.

"Whatever!" Barb giggled. "If you hit the lights, I'll set the alarm. Then you can have your ranger walk you home."

"Hm. My ranger." Rayna whispered to herself as she hit the light switch. "I can dream."

Outside, Wolf was waving at Fieldman and Sam who were both leaving the school's back lot. Rayna noticed that he was now wearing his gun, and she didn't recall seeing that on him earlier in the evening, much less during their time in the caves. Or, she thought, maybe she just didn't notice it earlier. Barb also noted the appearance of his gun and gave Rayna a tap on her good arm. "Looks like he was serious about nobody else hurting you," she whispered.

Rayna took a deep breath. "You might be right," she exhaled. "He rarely shows that thing whether he's wearing it, or not."

They watched Wolf lock his Jeep. His back was turned to them, and his shirt was tucked into his uniform pants, showing off a very nice backside. "Hm…" Barb whispered. "Gotta love a guy in uniform."

"Hush," Rayna elbowed her with her left arm, and Barb looked at her with one eyebrow raised. "Yeah, I do," Rayna admitted. "I really do."

Now they were within earshot of Wolf, and Barb spoke louder, "Well, I have to be on my way. I must be at work bright and early!" She nodded at Wolf. "You keep an eye on her, ya hear?"

"Yes, ma'am." He tilted his head to her. "I plan to."

Barb couldn't help herself and gave Rayna an obvious wink. "Don't stay up too late, now!"

Rayna shook her head. "No problem there. I'm exhausted."

Barb frowned. She worried that her friend might be about to sleep her way through what might be the most exciting night of her life. She stole a moment when Wolf looked at Rayna to mouth the words "Don't be stupid." And Rayna cracked a smile and touched Wolf's arm to show him the way to her house. While they were walking away from Barb, Rayna turned her head to look behind them and mouthed the phrase "I'm an idiot" back at her. Then Barb got in her car and left the lot and her friends behind.

The school parking lot was poorly lit in the summer time, when most people had no need to be there. The sun was down and the sky was clear with the nearly full moon and plenty of stars to give a soft glow to the old building and the rest of the town. Jupiter could really look magical on nights like this – like something out of a Thomas Kinkade painting. Warm lights glowed from within the houses that dotted the street leading toward her own at the edge of town. A quiet breeze whispered through the trees and the crickets and tree frogs were echoing their chorus throughout the valley.

Rayna was enjoying the moment, and it reminded her of why she chose to move back to a small mountain town to start her business when she left television. It was quiet, tranquil, even peaceful most of the time. This summer's events had been so unusual that she'd almost forgotten how charming Jupiter could be. For that instant, walking side by side with a handsome man toward her cute little house near the end of a quiet street, she felt blissful, and she assured herself it wasn't the pain meds making her feel that way.

When she noticed the unmarked, dark car with government plates parked at the end of her street, she realized that the FBI agents were making good on their promise of security until they found Hampton, or whatever his name was. She really hadn't given it any thought when they offered, and she didn't believe they'd do it. She figured they were the only two agents in the area. Apparently, she was mistaken. She raised her chin toward the vehicle. "The feds said they'd keep an eye on my place just in case."

Wolf regarded the car and the two strangers sitting inside it as they walked past. "I don't *have* to work tomorrow," he said. "I could stay if you'd rather have company than surveillance."

Rayna's pride answered before her head could process the offer. "I should be fine, but I appreciate it."

Wolf stopped walking and faced her, so she did the same. "I know you *should* be fine," he told her, "but I want to be sure that you *will* be."

She looked up into those mesmerizing blue eyes, which seemed to show even brighter in the light of the full moon, especially against his dark tan skin and dark hair. For a second, she was entranced. When she found the voice to speak, her own words surprised her. "I will be fine."

"Okay," he looked disappointed, but didn't lower his gaze.

"But..."

"But?" he repeated.

"I'd be a fool to say 'no'," she whispered.

Wolf put his hands on her waist and gently pulled her closer. The energy between the two of them was electric and it took Rayna's breath away. His eyes seemed even bluer somehow, and when she did finally inhale, she could smell that manly, almost woodsy, smell that seemed to be a part of the ranger uniform. He smelled like they beautiful mountain world they lived in. She inhaled more deeply and thought she might be lightheaded for a moment.

His hands squeezed her waste a little tighter. "Let me stay," he whispered, and he leaned down and gently pressed his lips to hers. Rayna pressed back and the gentle peck on the lips became something much more passionate.

To her own surprise, she didn't faint from the intensity, but she was breathless again. She pulled away from him, took a sharp breath, and smiled. "Please, stay."

Chapter 22

Something was buzzing in Rayna's room. As annoying as it was, she didn't want to open her eyes to figure it out. The buzz would pause for a second and then happen again. She narrowed the direction down to her bedside table before she finally opened her eyes to see what she was about to slam her hand down on to make it stop. Then she painfully realized that she couldn't slam her hand down on anything, not her right hand anyway. The initial motion to move her arm sent a shockwave from her fingers to her shoulder. "Oh!" she winced. "Damn!" The thing buzzed again, and she realized it was her cell phone, still on vibrate from the night before.

Her arm hurt, her head was fuzzy, and her eyes were bleary, but she made out the name on the screen when she sat upright and stared at it. "Really?" She asked the buzzing phone. With a big yawn, she laid back down on her left side and closed her eyes. A few minutes later, it was vibrating again. "Really?" she repeated and pushed herself back up into a seated position. She grabbed the phone with her left hand, but even that somehow reminded her that her right arm was throbbing again. "Hello?"

"Rayna?" Barb asked.

"Hey, Barb," she answered. Her voice was rough, and her throat felt dry.

"Hey! I'm just checking on you."

"Really? Why?"

There was a pause. "Your truck wasn't in your driveway," her friend finally answered.

"Right. It's at Sam's, remember?"

"Yeah, I guess. Are you… okay?"

Rayna was getting a little irritated. "As okay as I can be, sure. I was actually asleep."

"Oh," Barb said quietly. "Alone?"

"What?"

"Are you alone?"

Rayna rolled her eyes and wished her friend could see the action from the other side of the phone call. "There's no one else in my bed if that's what you're asking. Why?"

"Well, I was driving to work and saw your truck wasn't in the driveway. Then I passed the school and saw that Wolf's Jeep was still in the same place as last night. So, I was wondering… is he with you, or did he go missing, too?"

"You just happened to drive passed the back lot of the school, which requires you driving through the front lot of the school and around the building?"

There was another pause on Barb's end. "Um… yes."

Rayna looked at her closed door and wondered if she was about to tell the truth or just make an educated guess. "He's here."

Barb's excitement was audible. "Really! You said you were alone!"

Rayna's annoyance was growing. "No, I said there's no one in bed with me. He slept on the couch. At least, I think he did."

Barb's voice shrank. "So, nothing happened?"

"I didn't say that either."

"So, something happened?" The excitement was back.

Rayna sighed loudly. "Barb, I'll talk to you later."

"What? Why?"

"You woke me, and you've kept me on the phone long enough to realize that I need to take a pain killer for my arm, which means I need coffee and breakfast. So, I'm going to let you go now."

"But…"

"I'll talk to you later," she said firmly.

"Promise?"

"We'll see," Rayna answered and ended the call.

Sometimes she didn't understand what Barb was thinking. They'd been best friends for decades, and yet, occasionally, Barb still acted like she was a school girl. It was as if she hadn't outgrown the need for juicy gossip and the scoop before anyone else got the news. Heck! She was worse than Sam, and he was a journalist! All Rayna wanted was some uninterrupted sleep and a little privacy, and even her bestie couldn't give her that when she needed it most.

Rayna was so mad at Barb that she wasn't watching where she was going, and she nearly tripped over Cloud in the hallway. The cat meowed loudly and ran toward the living room ahead of her. The little black fur ball stopped right in front of the couch and flicked her tail as if to remind Rayna that a guest had taken one of her favorite spots.

Wolf had indeed slept on the couch. He was still lying there with his forearm covering his eyes and a fleece throw covering him from the waist down with not a hint of fabric in between. Rayna's heart skipped a beat at the sight. He was definitely in the kind of shape she imagined under those green button-down uniform shirts. Man! He looked amazing.

"Is everything okay?" His words surprised her. He moved his arm away from his face to show that he was fully awake and probably very aware that she had been standing there nearly drooling over him.

Rayna shook herself out of her dumbfounded moment and cleared her throat. "Yes, Barb was just being... well... Barb. She can be a bit nosey sometimes." Rayna fought the urge to sit down on the couch beside him and instead headed through the room toward the kitchen. "Do you want some coffee?" She glanced back at the couch in time to see him sit up and feet hit the floor. "Darn!" she thought. He still had his pants on.

Wolf stretched and answered, "yes, please!"

"How about breakfast?" She called from the kitchen.

"What do you have?"

She heard the sofa squeak when he stood and then his socked footfalls following her into the kitchen. "Let's see." She opened the cupboard door where she usually kept the breakfast foods and was embarrassed to realize it was empty. She opened another and answered, "brown rice, a jar of olives, and a box of yellow cake mix." She turned to face him. "I just remembered I was planning on grocery shopping after our little excursion to the caves yesterday. What?"

He was grinning at her from ear to ear. "You're worse than I am." He took a couple steps closer to her, and she was sure she could feel the heat from his body warming hers. No wonder he slept with his shirt off.

"Sorry," she answered while trying not to stare at his ripped, tan chest and stomach. "Getting shot kind of threw my plan for the day off a little." She leaned back on the counter because she had that feeling again that her knees might buckle if he came any closer, and he did come closer.

She looked down at her feet and suddenly became very aware of what she was wearing. Her anger at Barb and the shock of seeing Wolf shirtless had kept her from thinking about it. She was in her bare feet, the same khaki pants, and t-shirt she'd worn to the school the night before. She didn't remember taking her socks off, but she was half sorry that she was still wearing the same clothes. "Wait a minute," she said. "How did I end up in my bed last night?" Everything was still fuzzy. She remembered they sat on the couch and talked and kissed and then what?

He chuckled. "After you took that medicine, we sat and talked for a while. Then we did a little more than talking." Rayna raised an eyebrow at him, and he put his hands up in that universal sign for "I didn't do anything wrong." "We just kissed, and well... not just kissed... but... um... I mean... I really enjoyed it. The kissing, I mean." She cracked a smile. Was he really at a loss for words? He was still struggling. "Yeah, I mean… Anyway, you sort of passed out. Mid-kiss."

Rayna put her hands to her mouth and gasped. Wolf started laughing. "It's okay!" he assured her. "I know, or at least I hope, it was just the meds."

She looked down at her feet again and rubbed her eyes. "Oh, dear Lord," she said and started giggling quietly, and then a little louder.

"Yeah, you were just kind of done. Right then and there." He closed the short distance left between them and kissed her on the cheek. She could feel herself blush. He stroked her dark hair and pulled her bangs away from her eyes. "It was kind of funny in a pathetic way." Great. Just great. She finally got the man of her dreams to spend the night and nothing happened, even worse – she fell asleep while kissing him. How was that even possible? He kissed her forehead. "It's okay," he said. "The doctor told you those things would knock you out."

She didn't lift her eyes from the floor. "So, you put me to bed?"

"I did," he answered. "When you didn't answer my calling your name several times, but you still had a pulse – yes, I checked," he chuckled again. "I picked you up as gently as I could and carried you into the bedroom. I took off your socks, but that was it. I put the sheets over you, closed the door and came out here to camp on the couch for the night."

She finally looked back up into those smiling, deep blue eyes. "I guess I should apologize and thank you for being such a gentleman."

"No thanks necessary. I did what I came here to do," he winked. "I took you to bed."

Rayna lost her composure and finally started laughing. "Oh my God! You did!" She threw her hands up in the air and winced in pain. "Ouch! Darn!" The jolt killed her laughter. "I forgot I'm not supposed to do that."

"It hurts, huh?"

"Yes, and I can't take medicine on an empty stomach."

"Why don't we go have breakfast in town?"

She smiled at him. "That's definitely more appealing than yellow cake topped with green olives. Ew!"

"Go change your clothes, and remember that sling, young lady." He said and kissed her forehead again. Then he stepped away from her and grinned. "There's no way I'm kissing you on the lips again until I am sure you'll stay awake for it."

She wanted to assure him that she was wide awake at that moment, but the idea of morning breath kept her quiet. She'd wait until she could give him the kind of kiss that would erase the memory of her sleeping through their last one, if that was even possible. As she watched him walk back into the living room, she decided to make that a goal. "I really need a shower, but I'm not sure how to do it without getting this wound wet. It might take me a minute to figure it out. Do you mind waiting?" she asked and watched him button his shirt.

"Not at all. I'd offer to help, but you might think it was for the wrong reasons."

She wondered if any reason could be wrong where he was concerned. "Yeah... any suggestions then?"

"Where do you keep your plastic bags?"

"In the kitchen," she answered.

He walked back into the kitchen and she followed and pointed to the cabinet under the sink. "And some tape?"

"I have duct tape in that drawer." She pointed to the one to his right.

He carefully used a bag to cover her arm and duct taped it tight above and below the wound. "That ought to work. I'll help you cut it off when you're done."

"Thanks," she said. I'll be back in a few. You can watch TV, or read, or whatever. You know where my library is."

He smiled. "Yes, I do."

Chapter 23

The little shiny diner was busy, even for a Sunday morning. Wolf held the door open for Rayna who stopped short as soon as she walked in. There were no empty tables. The booths were full, even the one with the broken bench, and the counter was crowded. She looked across the street at the lesser favored diner. Wolf said, "don't bother," as if reading her mind, and he pointed to a table where a father and son were putting on their jackets, preparing to leave.

In a small town, everyone looks familiar whether you know them personally, or not. So, when the father flashed a stiff, but friendly smile at Rayna as he stood to leave, she didn't think much of it. She just smiled back and started walking toward the soon to be empty table. He was about six feet, four inches tall and on the heavy side, like a football lineman who had stopped working out. His sandy hair was cropped close to his head and his denim jacket was dusty and stained. Rayna imagined he worked on a farm somewhere nearby.

His son was a pipsqueak in comparison, a pint-sized six-year-old with his father's haircut and big, green eyes. The son addressed her first. "What happened to your arm?" he asked pointing at Rayna's sling.

Rayna smiled at the child and said, "it got hurt yesterday."

"Did a space man shoot it with his ray gun?" the child asked excitedly.

Rayna stopped walking, looked down at the little boy and then up at his father, who avoided eye contact. She stepped aside to let the two of them pass so she could get to the table. The little boy followed his father past her and Wolf, but never took his eyes off her sling. "No, sir," she finally answered. "There was no ray gun involved."

The girl behind the counter snickered. The father told his son to "hush" and headed quickly for the register. Rayna and Wolf made themselves comfortable and waited for the table to be cleaned.

"That was interesting," Wolf said, watching the little boy who kept looking back at them.

"It's a small town," Rayna replied. "The spooky weather woman has once again provided fodder for its gossip."

"You're not 'spooky,'" he smiled at her. "Well, not always."

She grinned back. "So, Ranger Wolf, do I scare you?"

"Not at all."

"Ask her, Daddy!" They heard the same child pleading with his father. "Just ask her, please!"

Rayna looked over to see the big man walking back toward her table. "Um, ma'am," he hesitated.

"Was there a spaceman?" the little boy blurted out. Wolf laughed, and the father's neck and face turned a bright shade of red.

Rayna questioned the child, "why would you ask that?"

"Because we – my daddy and me – we saw a UFO!"

"Really?" Wolf asked.

"Really!" the little guy answered earnestly.

"Really?" Rayna repeated, looking at his dad.

"Well," the father started to speak and rubbed the back of his neck. "We might have. I mean I've never seen anything like it before."

"What did it look like?" she asked.

The man looked around nervously. Suddenly, the whole diner was quiet. Rayna saw the problem. He didn't want to be judged. It was fine for her to be the subject of gossip, but he had probably spent most of his life avoiding it. Rayna looked at the people around her. "Breakfast and a show, huh?" The ones who had been watching went back to eating, but they didn't go back to talking amongst themselves. They wanted to listen. Rayna smiled, took out a pen, and wrote her cell number on a napkin. "I'd love to hear the details. Please call me after you leave here." She handed the napkin to him, and he took it with a nod. Then he took his son by the hand, turned and left.

"Do you think he'll call?" Wolf asked while watching them exit the diner.

"Yes," she answered frankly.

"Why?"

"Because his curiosity and the need for an explanation will get the best of him."

"Hopefully, he calls before his wife finds your phone number written on a napkin in his jacket pocket."

Rayna chuckled. "Right. That would be good."

A young waitress walked up to the table, "Would y'all like some coffee?"

"Definitely," Rayna answered, and glanced up to see a new face at her favorite diner. The girl was about nineteen with brown hair pulled back in a tight ponytail. She seemed to have way too much makeup on for waiting tables in Jupiter, but Rayna decided that she was young enough to think it was appropriate.

"Do you know what you wanna eat?" Her green eyes focused on Rayna intently.

Wolf nodded, and Rayna said, "sausage biscuit and gravy, please."

The girl glanced at Wolf momentarily, but her eyes were back on Rayna when she asked, "and you, sir?"

"I'll have a short stack with a side of bacon," he answered.

"No one can accuse you of eating healthy," a voice said from behind the waitress, who turned quickly around to see the sheriff standing there. She shuffled around him as quickly as she could while avoiding eye contact with him. "May I join you for a minute?" he asked, pointing at the bench on which Rayna was sitting.

She answered, "yes, sir," and scooted closer to the wall. She thought about Wolf's Jeep parked outside. You can always find someone in a small town if you know what vehicle to look for. "To what do I owe this pleasure?"

"I just wanted to check on you, Rayna. I had a very interesting conversation with Barb a few minutes ago. She filled me in on what I somehow got left out of yesterday." He had a stern look on his face and concern in his voice while he looked back and forth between Rayna and Wolf. "I'm wondering if there's anything else I need to know."

"Most of yesterday's excitement happened on Park Service land. It wasn't your jurisdiction." Wolf said it as respectfully as he could.

"Most?" The sheriff asked.

Rayna nodded. "The most important part, yes."

"And what of the men in black you that met you at the hospital?" Suddenly the room went silent again as all ears alerted to the sheriff's voice.

Aware of the audience, Rayna said loudly, "They were not men in black. They were FBI." She made eye contact with a few of the nosey people around her so that they'd realize they were not invited into the conversation. Each one looked down at his or her plate, embarrassed. Then she lowered her voice and looked the sheriff in the eyes, "I told Barb they were FBI. She didn't tell you?"

"Either she didn't believe them, or she doesn't believe you. We have federal agents in my town, and I didn't know anything about it. I don't like that."

The waitress brought the coffee to the table and hesitated. She took a second to work up the nerve to ask the sheriff if he cared for coffee or a menu. He answered "no" firmly and she looked relieved. Rayna wondered what else she did besides waiting tables at the diner that would cause fear of interaction with law enforcement. This was the first time she'd seen the server before. In fact, the girl didn't look familiar at all.

"Dean," Rayna used his first name for effect, "I'm sorry that you feel we left you out of the loop, but it was not purposeful. Everything happened very quickly yesterday. Besides, I knew Barb would fill you in."

"And you know that sometimes what I get from Barb and what actually happened are slightly different things. If you would be so kind, I would appreciate a visit to my office when you are through here." The sheriff stood while he was speaking.

"Should I come, too?" The ranger asked.

Dean shrugged. "It's up to you. I trust Rayna to give me pertinent details, however since 'most' of the events happened on your watch, whatever the Park Service would like to share is appreciated." He tipped his brown hat to the two of them and left.

Wolf smirked at Rayna. "What?" she asked.

"Breakfast with you is always exciting, isn't it?"

"No," she laughed. "I feel like I just got called into the principal's office."

"Do you want me to go with you?"

"No, you can go to work and see about finding that so-called professor." She frowned at the thought of the jerk. He was probably three states away by now, but she had to hope that someone would catch him. Sure it was just a mild wound compared to what it could have been, but it still hurt. The thought reminded her to take the medicine she had put in her purse.

She was pulling the bottle out when she heard "Here's your food." The waitress was standing beside the table with two plates heaped with their breakfasts. "Need anything else?" she asked and laid the plates down in front of them.

"No, thanks," Wolf answered. Rayna just shook her head. The waitress walked away. "Did that seem unusual to you?" he asked her.

Rayna understood his meaning immediately. "Yes, how long had she been there? It's like she was in stealth mode. People can't usually sneak up on me."

"Ever seen her before?" he asked while watching the girl ring someone up at the register.

"Never."

"Hmm…" he rubbed his chin. "Weird."

"Very," Rayna became aware of music, a piano riff that sounded awfully similar to "Bad to the Bone," coming out of her purse. She took the phone out of it and saw an unfamiliar number. "I don't know this one," she told him. "I'm sorry. I feel like I should take it." She tapped the phone. "Hello?"

The voice on the other end was vaguely familiar. "Hello, Rayna?"

"Yes."

"This is Bob, the guy from the diner this morning."

"Hi, Bob, I'm glad you called." Rayna tried to motion to Wolf to let him know who it was, but he was too busy eating. She looked down at her food. It looked delicious. She knew it wouldn't be as good if she let it get cold."

"I do want to talk to you about what we, my son and me, saw," Bob explained. "I just couldn't do it in the diner, you know?"

"Yes, I do," she said with a mouthful of biscuit.

There was a pause, and Bob finally asked, "are you still at the diner?"

Rayna swallowed. "Yes, our food just arrived."

"I... I'm sorry to bother you."

"No, no bother, really, if you don't mind my eating while you tell me about it."

"No, ma'am. You eat. I'll talk."

"Okay." Rayna shoveled another forkful in her mouth.

"See, we were down at the river camping out and fishing last weekend. It was getting kind of dark, so I was trying to get a fire started. My boy was wishing on every star he could see. You know how kids are."

"I do."

"So, he starts yelling 'Daddy! Daddy! Look at this!' and I looked up. He was pointing toward the west, I think. I watched as this thing, huge and full of green, red, and white lights got closer. At first, it was far away and I couldn't tell how big it was. I tried to tell him it was a plane even though it wasn't, and I knew it. Well, it kept coming toward us and looking bigger and bigger. I grabbed my boy and got into the tent 'cause I didn't know what else to do. I tell you, ma'am, when that thing went over us, it was at least as big as a football stadium, and the craziest thing about it was there was *no noise*!"

"Totally silent?" Rayna asked between bites.

"Totally! It was the creepiest thing I've ever seen!"

"Did it stop like it noticed you?"

"No. Thank the Lord, no! It kept right on going, kind of following the river south."

Rayna tried to keep her voice down but repeat the basics loud enough for Wolf to hear because at that point, he had deduced who was on the phone and was paying attention. "So, it was big, moved slowly, and no noise? At what speed would you guess it was moving?"

Bob answered after a moment of thought. "Maybe ten miles an hour. For as big as it was, it seemed like it ought to just fall out of the sky at that rate. I mean, I know how airplanes work, and it takes air speed to keep them in the air."

"Are you sure it wasn't a blimp?"

"No. No, it wasn't a blimp. It was too dang big to be a blimp, and rounder, much rounder. "It really was the size of a football stadium!"

"Can you tell me anything else about it?"

"Only that I never want to see it again!"

Rayna thanked him for calling her and assured him that she'd let him know if she found anything out about it. Wolf watched as she hung up her phone and slid it into her purse. She looked at him and smiled. "That was Bob," she whispered.

"Bob?" He mouthed the name silently with a quizzical look.

"The big man with the little boy," she spoke quietly and looked around. Most of the diners who had been near them had left by then. The place was almost empty.

"I guessed that was who it was."

"I'll fill you in later." She nodded at the few people left in the place.

The two finished their breakfast and parted ways after Wolf drove Rayna to the Sheriff's Office.

Barb's eyes were huge when she saw Rayna being dropped off at the doors of the office by the handsome ranger in his Jeep. She stared at her friend who awkwardly opened the passenger door with her left hand and looked back toward Wolf to say goodbye. "Go on, kiss him," Barb whispered. Apparently, Rayna didn't hear her through the glass doors. She closed the vehicle door behind her and waved goodbye to him. Rayna had barely walked through those glass doors before she was bombarded with questions.

"He's not coming in?" Barb sounded disappointed.

"No."

"But he spent the night?"

"On the couch," Rayna wanted to make sure any prying ears heard that little factoid.

"So, nothing happened?"

"No."

Barb raised an eyebrow. "No, nothing happened, or no, something happened?"

"Barb..." Rayna was torn between being annoyed and amused by her friend.

"Rayna," the sheriff's loud voice interrupted. "Thank you for coming so promptly!" He was standing in the doorway to his office to the left of the reception desk where Barb sat.

Rayna was grateful for the interruption. "No problem, sheriff! I just had to get a ride here." She pointed to her sling. "This thing will make driving difficult."

"I understand. I'll have one of my deputies drive you home when we're finished here."

"Thank you, sir." Rayna followed him into his office and took a seat in the chair in front of his desk.

He shut the door to his office and sat in his own, much more comfortable looking chair and leaned back in it. "First off, how is your arm?" He asked earnestly with a voice softer than normal.

Rayna looked down at her boring, beige sling. "It's okay, just hurts when I move it. The pain meds help."

"What did they put you on?"

"Some long-named thing that I'm only taking before bed. I opted for prescription strength acetaminophen this morning, so I could think clearly, and even that is making me drowsier than I should be after three cups of coffee."

"And diner coffee, no less! That stuff could keep a sloth going for days." He chuckled to himself. Rayna gave a half smile. She wasn't used to the sheriff trying to be light-hearted. He was usually pretty serious when he was in uniform. "That's why I like you, Rayna," he continued. "You have some sense about you." He gave her a quick wink. "You don't panic. You look at things rationally, and you're a good observer."

Rayna was a little surprised by the compliments. "Um, thank you, Dean."

"There are reasons I don't mind sharing – shall we say – investigative territory with you." He leaned forward and rested his arms on the desk with his hands clasped. "You look into the paranormal and leave the so-called 'normal' to us."

"Yes, sir." Rayna felt a "but" coming.

"This time, it seems you and I need to be in communication a little more than usual. This time, our investigations are truly overlapping. This time I need to know *everything* you're finding."

Rayna was feeling a little less than comfortable. "Yes, sir," is all she could come up with. He was right. The mundane things that had cropped up during the investigation were definitely in his jurisdiction. He had every right to know. It's not like she was hiding anything. She was just so used to doing her own thing that she hadn't thought to clue him in. The more she thought about it, she was surprised that Barb hadn't once said "don't you think we should tell the sheriff?" Not that she was blaming Barb for her lack of consideration, but it was unusual.

"So," Dean leaned in a little farther and locked eyes with her. His eyes were blue-gray and gentler than you'd expect from a man of his stature. She suddenly felt a little more at ease. "From the beginning, that first day on the farm with the dead horse, tell me everything."

Rayna leaned back in her chair and told him every detail that she could remember as chronologically as she could. It felt good to put it all out there for an objective person to hear. Maybe Dean would find connections, or answers even, where she and her friends could not. While she knew some of the more mundane things could be explained by the undercover professor's rogue agent status, there were too many other things that didn't fit that narrative. In fact, the horse, the green flashes during the unexplained blackout, the UFOs that she and Wolf witnessed together, and the larger one that Bob had just told her he'd seen didn't fit with the "agent turned bad" story at all. Rayna expressed that concern when she was finished telling the sheriff about that morning's run in with Bob and the phone call that followed.

"You're right," the sheriff said. "It doesn't all fit together nicely."

"And we still don't know what happened to Lee when he disappeared. He has no memory of that time. Plus, my laptop is gone. If the person who took Lee and the laptop, assuming it was a person, is the same one that broke into my house, what was he looking for, and why did he think I would have it?"

"I wonder if those guys from the FBI would know anything about that."

"I didn't even think to ask them. Do you think Hampton had anything to do with it?"

"There are certain things we can chalk up to people and other things we still have no reasonable explanations for. A person broke into your house. A person shot at you. A person is using the caves in Bell Mountain, probably to hide his activities. I'm pretty sure a person has your laptop, and I'd like to think a person is responsible for Lee's disappearance and reappearance even though he remembers nothing."

"But what about the odd shape in the grass near where his car was found and the weird K-2 readings inside it?"

The sheriff paused. "That could be completely coincidental. Your ranger said he'd never noticed it before, but had he ever been looking for it?" Rayna noted his use of "your ranger" and her mind started to drift for a second. That ranger wasn't hers yet, but the idea didn't seem as foreign as it did just twenty-four hours earlier. Dean was still talking. "Without someone who can definitively say they were there the day before and saw that there were absolutely no weird markings in the grass at that spot, I can't assume they appeared at the same time Lee's car was... arrived at that spot."

The sheriff had a good point. How often had Rayna gotten mad at others for jumping to conclusions based on evidence that was circumstantial at best? "You're right," she admitted. "There's no way to know when the markings appeared."

"So, now, about your missing time?"

"Missing time?" Rayna was baffled.

"Didn't you say that you arrived at the parking lot on Bell Mountain much later than you should have the night of the blackout?"

"Yes, but..."

"You weren't trying to tell me something more?"

"No, I mean... I don't think there's more to tell." Rayna was suddenly uncomfortable again. She shifted in her chair, looked down at the sling on her right arm, and tried to pull her thoughts together.

"Rayna," the sheriff pressed her, "just how long do you think you were stopped on the side of the road trying to figure out what you saw?"

"Maybe it was longer than it felt."

"Okay, then. How long did it feel?"

Rayna didn't like where this was going. There had been something about the incident nagging at her since that night, but she'd been busy enough to keep it out of her mind most of the time. When it did creep into her thoughts, she refused to let herself dwell on it. She sighed quietly and raised her brown eyes to meet the sheriff's. "it didn't feel like more than five minutes at most."

"Were you driving five miles an hour to get there?"

Rayna exhaled sharply. "No, sir."

"Then, it sounds to me like you're missing time. You said that you never got out of the car?"

"Right. I wanted to, but my nerves got the better of me and I stayed put."

"Are you sure?"

"Absolutely!" she insisted. Rayna knew it didn't make sense, but she also knew she had chickened out of leaving the safety of the truck to investigate. "For the first time since I was a child, I chickened out."

The sheriff nodded and grinned. "I'd call it 'playing it safe.' You still don't carry a firearm, right?"

"Right," she nodded her head.

"Staying in the vehicle was the right thing to do." He assured her.

"Honestly, after all of this, I'm starting to think a conceal and carry permit isn't a bad idea." Rayna had only considered owning a gun in passing. She didn't mind guns, but she hadn't seen a need for one until that moment.

"It might be a good idea, but only if you take the safety classes and feel completely comfortable using a weapon. I have plenty of deputies here that could and would like to help you out with that." Dean smiled at her. The benefit to being well-known in town was that most of the deputies liked Rayna and even the married ones tried to spend time with her. "Or," he continued, "I'm sure that ranger friend of yours could take care of you." He winked.

"Maybe, but I prefer to take care of myself," she quipped.

"Yes, ma'am." The sheriff took the hint. "Well, Miss Rayna, I think we're about done here. Shall I ask one of my deputies to take you home?"

Rayna looked out the window at the sundrenched, tree-lined street. Her house was only a half-mile away, and the thought of fresh air made her smile. "No, thank you, Sheriff. I think I'll walk."

"As you wish," he replied and walked her out of his office. "You have your cell phone with you, correct?"

"Yes, sir." She patted her purse to let him know the phone was inside.

"Don't hesitate to use it."

"I won't, Dean. Thank you."

The sheriff left her in the lobby and she looked around for Barb, but her friend wasn't at her post. She found a post-it stack and a pen and left a note on the reception desk that said, "Call me! I'll spill it!" and left the building.

Outside on the front walk, a middle-aged, blonde deputy stopped her. "Hey, Miss Rayna! Can I give you a lift?" He was tall with brown eyes and a pleasant, but stiff smile.

"Hi, Charles." She paused and pointed in the direction of her house. "I'm fine. I'm just less than a mile that way and I could use the fresh air from a walk. I appreciate the offer though!"

"Are you sure?" He was insistent. "I don't mind. I'm not sure you should be alone right now."

"What?" She furled her eyebrows.

"I just mean that I heard what happened, and they haven't caught the guy yet, right?"

"Right," she looked down at her sling. She really needed to stop wearing it. It was more of an attraction, the wrong kind of attraction, than an aid in her mind. "No," she sighed, "they haven't as far as I know."

"I'd be happy to drive you home and keep an eye on things for you." His eagerness actually made her uneasy. Was he worried about her, nosey, or was it some odd way of hitting on her? After what Dean had said about having so many deputies willing to teach her how to handle a gun, she wasn't sure anymore about Charles's kindness over the years. It wasn't that he was unattractive. He was actually pretty good looking for a man thirteen years her senior. He just wasn't her type and was older than she wanted to date.

"No, really, Charles, I'm good." He looked like he wasn't going to take "no" for an answer, so she added, "I think Sam is bringing my truck to me in an hour, or so. I doubt anything other than a nap is going to happen by then."

"A nap?" he looked confused.

"Yes," she nodded. "The pain medicine makes me sleepy, and I just want to get some fresh air and then relax on my sofa."

"Ah, alright then." He deflated a bit, but then perked right back up. "You know how to reach me if you need me!"

"Yes, yes, I do." She answered.

He stepped to the side and let her pass with a quick tip of his hat. She wondered if he was on that list the sheriff had in mind of his men that wanted to help her, and if so, how long he had been there. How many were there? Who else was on it? The thought of missing out on a potential romance because she had been too blind to see that someone was interested nagged at her. Had she been lonely for so long for no reason? Then she thought about the guys she knew on the force. Nobody exceptionally attractive to her came to mind. Most of the cute ones her age had already married, or worse, dated Barb. She could never date anyone that had gone out with her best friend. It would be just too weird, but not any weirder than dating Lee would be. Yeah, there was a reason she was still single. She decided she was better off not knowing who was interested in her at the Sheriff's Office. It would just make interactions with them awkward, and she didn't want that.

Once she put the thought of lost romantic opportunities to rest, her mind went back to her talk with the sheriff. She actually felt a little relieved after having laid out everything she knew to an objective third party with a keen investigator's sense. Her brain buzzed with possible links and explanations for all of the events of the past several weeks. Were the mystery hums and cheap fireworks on Bell Mountain somehow related to the rogue FBI agent's odd behavior? Or did those strange occurrences have something to do with the UFO sightings? Maybe none of it was related and she and her friends were trying to find connections that didn't exist.

The ring of her cell phone interrupted her thoughts as she turned the corner on her street. "Hello?" she answered.

"Miss Smith?" a male voice asked.

"This is she."

"This is Agent Black. I thought you would like to know that we picked up Hampton just a little while ago in Virginia."

There was sincere relief in Rayna's voice when she asked, "you did?"

"Yes, ma'am." His tone, by comparison, was flat.

"So, what happens now?"

"He will be questioned thoroughly, and we'll be in touch."

Rayna's response was slow to form. "Okay... I have some questions of my own."

"We'll be in touch," Black repeated. The hang-up immediately followed.

"I have some questions of my own for him." Rayna said to her phone, disappointed the words didn't form more quickly. "Dammit." She sighed deeply, and then dialed the sheriff to give him an update.

"I would guess you're not going to get much out of them, Rayna." The sheriff told her. "Unless they need more from you, they'll probably try to keep this quiet and handle it internally."

"That's what I'm afraid of," she confided.

"Unfortunately," he continued, "I can't do much to help with them since the shooting was not in my jurisdiction."

"That's okay, Dean. I just wanted to give you a heads up." When she ended the call, his words made her pause. He was right. The shooting wasn't in his jurisdiction. It was in Wolf's. The rangers may have some say, or some insight into why Hampton was hiding in the caves now that they'd had time to investigate. They might even be working with the FBI on it. As much as she knew Sam, Barb, and Fieldman would want to know that the man who injured her was arrested, she decided to call the only one who might have found some answers next. She had to talk with Wolf.

She dialed his number and it went straight to voicemail. Of course, it did! He was on duty and that was his personal number. She felt stupid and verbally stumbled through her reason for calling, or at least she though she did. "Hi, Wolf, it's me, Rayna. I just got a call from the FBI – Agent Black, actually. He says the caught Hampton in Virginia this morning. I was hoping you could help me... with answers. I mean getting answers about what he was up to in the caves... Anyway, I guess... call when you can. Please. Bye."

She always felt silly leaving voicemails because they weren't expected or rehearsed. They were just her trying to sum up why she called, and even though she had a legitimate reason for calling him, she was still disappointed simply because she didn't hear his live voice answer her call. A recording just wasn't good enough. She had just seen him a few hours before and she was already missing his voice? "Ugh," she said quietly while unlocking her front door. "I can't have it that badly." Yet, in her heart, she knew she did.

Chapter 24

"Surely there must be something you can tell me about the rumors that they're making tritium up there." Sam was on his phone when he arrived to check on Rayna. "So, you think it's possible?" He gave her a smile when she opened her kitchen door to let him in. "Yeah? That would be much appreciated. Yes, of course. Strictly off the record." His grin expanded. "Thank you, Moyra." He ended the call and followed Rayna to the living room where she sat on the sofa and he plopped down in her recliner.

"Are you finally getting somewhere?" She asked.

"No clue." His answer didn't match the smile on his face.

"Then why the big grin?"

"Because Moyra from the DOE is sending me the only document she can find related to testing for potential tritium leaks up the river." He leaned toward his friend for emphasis. "The tests were apparently done three months ago."

"Really?" Rayna understood the grin. "Why test if they weren't considering doing it again, right?"

"Or if they weren't already doing it?" Sam sat back. "That's my thinking."

"It's better than nothing," Rayna said hopefully. "Let's see. We've been working this case for what? About a month now?"

"Since our first trip to the farm, yes."

"That would be two months after testing." She thought out loud. "Long enough for them to start and want to know if there was a leak and if it was going downstream, I guess?"

Sam rubbed his chin. "I guess. We'd have to ask someone else how long it would be between approval and implementation. Moyra was unsure."

"I wonder if Derek would know."

"Hm… not sure if a chemistry professor would be privy to DOE timelines and protocol, but I guess you could ask him." He straightened up in his seat again. "Have you talked to him since his officemate… um…"

"Shot me?" Rayna finished his thought. "No, I'm not even sure he knows about that. I guess I have another reason to call him."

"Do you think that guy shot you because you could identify him?"

"Probably. My guess is that he was too shocked at our presence to come up with a quick, believable reason for being there, so he panicked."

"I know how you feel about panic."

"It's a waste of energy," she sighed. "And bullets."

"You didn't panic when you saw that gun?"

"No," Rayna answered honestly. "I was horrified, but not panicked. We had an exit, or at least a direction to run, so I didn't feel as trapped as I might have otherwise."

"What about your jump into the river?" her friend asked. "I know how you hate heights and muddy water. Wolf guessed you were about forty feet up?"

"Yeah, but jumping into that water made more sense than staying there and waiting to see if the guy with the gun was following us."

Sam chuckled. "Yeah, you're right there."

"I guess when the adrenaline kicks in, the fear gets put on hold." She shrugged.

"So, you're still afraid of heights?"

She shrugged again. "I'm not in a hurry to find out."

Rayna's phone vibrated on the end table next to her. "It's Wolf," she told Sam. He noticed the tone in her voice change slightly when she answered. Instead of Rayna-sweet, it was almost sticky sweet. "Hi, Wolf," she said and caught the smirk on Sam's face. Sam immediately tilted his head down and batted his eyelashes at her to poke fun. She waved him off and turned her body so she was facing the kitchen to avoid any further distraction from him.

Wolf's voice was low and she could hear other men's voices in the background. "Hey, Rayna. I got your message, and yes, I've got some things to share with you, but not now."

She assumed from the context that the owners of those voices around him would frown on his sharing more info. "Okay," she said, "just say when."

"Can I come by after work tonight?" That question put an unexpected lump in her throat. Of course, he could! She'd love to see him again! Still, she wanted to play it cool, and she didn't want to assume he had anything other than an investigation-related reason to come by. Guys like him didn't stay interested in her for long, if they ever showed interest to begin with. She cleared her throat. "Yes, I'll be around. What time do you think it will be?"

"It might not be until after 8:30 or 9:00," he answered.

Out of the corner of her eye, she could see Sam shaking his pointed index finger as if warning her she was misbehaving. "That works for me," she replied to Wolf.

"Okay," he said. "I'll see you then, and I'll call when I'm on my way."

"Okay," she answered and heard the call click off. She put her phone down and turned to face Sam, who was still smirking at her. "What?" she demanded.

"You know what!" He said and wagged his finger at her again.

Rayna couldn't help but grin, and she started to laugh, but a thought stopped her. "Crap!" she slapped her thigh. "I still need to go grocery shopping!"

"Why, are you going to be a one-armed chef tonight? He's coming over, isn't he?"

She smiled again. "Yes, but not for dinner." There was that smirk again. Then Rayna realized what she'd said. "Shut up! Not for that either!"

"Uh-huh," her old friend teased her.

"Seriously, Sam! Do you think I'd jump from kissing to sex that quickly?" she put her left hand on her hip in mock anger.

Sam's eyes were huge. "You kissed him?"

Oops! Rayna didn't mean to share that little tidbit with him. Unlike Barb, Sam was very protective of her. Teasing aside, he'd threaten anyone who might hurt her, physically or emotionally. It was too late to take that question back, so she answered, "he kissed me first." Yeah, that sounded very grown up.

"When?"

"Last night after he walked me home."

"Just once?"

"No." She dropped her hand to her lap, but not her eyes.

"And he spent the night?" His tone was flat, not judgmental. He was being the curious interviewer his job required him to be even though this little story would never see print.

"On the couch," she answered firmly.

"And where did you sleep?"

"In my bed!" She stated emphatically. "I just said I don't move that fast!"

Sam chuckled and put his hands up, palms out, in a motion to calm her. "Okay, okay, there. Calm down. I was just asking. Don't want him to take advantage."

Rayna gave him a sly grin. "Well, maybe I did," she laughed, "but he didn't."

"So why is he coming over after dark tonight?" Sam prodded.

"He has info about my shooter he couldn't discuss over the phone."

"So, would it be okay if I were here for it, too?"

Rayna hesitated. Sure, technically it would be fine for Sam to be there, but she didn't want him there. "I guess," she finally answered, "but that doesn't mean you *should* be here."

"I see." He nodded. She was thankful that he took the hint. "In that case, I'll stay at home. I'm sure Cloud would be happy to chaperone in my place." The cat purred at the sound of her name.

"My sweet Cloud," Rayna said, looking at the little black ball of fur curled up on the floor near her feet. "Oh, crap!" Rayna sighed loudly. "I forgot she's almost out of food, too."

"Well, Dear," Sam stood, "Let's get you to a grocery store. It's one thing to starve yourself, and quite another to starve your feline friend."

Rayna stood as well. "Thanks for volunteering."

"No problem." He smiled. "I do what I can."

8:30pm came and went. Rayna drummed her fingers on her desk and tried not to watch the clock. Cloud sat on the leather pub chair across the room and stared at her as if the sound annoyed her. "Sorry!" Rayna apologized to the green-eyed cat who just blinked and looked away. "You'd be like this, too, if you could tell time," Rayna continued. The cat settled her head on her front paws and glanced at Rayna as if to say, "I doubt it."

Both heard a car pulling into her driveway just before a stream of headlights crossed the walls of the room. "I thought he said he'd call," Rayna told the cat who sat up when she heard the car door. The next thought that crossed Rayna's mind bothered her. "What if it's not him?" She grabbed her phone off the desk and walked to the window to peek between the blinds. Sure enough, there was Wolf's Jeep in her driveway. She breathed a sigh of relief.

Cloud beat her to the door and was standing there meowing at it. "Silly kitty!" Rayna said as she scooped the cat up with her good arm. Then she waited for a knock. She didn't want to seem too eager. After what seemed like an eternity, it finally came. She took a breath and opened the front door. Then her heart skipped a beat.

Wolf stood facing her, holding a pizza box in both hands with that gorgeous smile on his face. She had never seen him look so good. He was wearing faded blue jeans, a plain, dark blue t-shirt, and his hair was down. She'd realized it had always been in a braid, and he'd always had worn some version of a ranger uniform every time they'd seen each other. Tonight, he didn't look like a ranger. He was just a hot guy holding a pizza standing at her door, and she was smiling stupidly.

"Hi," he said.

"Hi," she exhaled.

"Um, can I come in?"

Rayna blushed at her rudeness. "I'm sorry. I..."

"I didn't call first," he interrupted. "I should have." She stepped aside to let him in. "I'm sorry," he said as he walked past her.

"No, it's fine! Really," she assured him.

"I was just really hungry and wanted to hurry up and get here." He stood in her hallway and raised the box a little. "Have you eaten?"

"Not much," she answered and pointed him to the kitchen. "I'll never pass up a personally delivered pizza."

"I got off work late, and really needed a shower first," he explained. "I'm sorry I'm a little late."

She looked at the clock on the stove that read 9:08. "You're not late. Stop apologizing." She grabbed two plates from the cabinet and set them on the table. He opened the box and her mouth watered.

"Veggie supreme from Antonino's down the valley," he told her. "I hope you're okay with it."

"Are you kidding?" She pointed to the pie. "That's my favorite!" She went to the refrigerator. "I went shopping today. I now have food again, and more importantly, beer. You want one?"

"Yes, please." He took a seat at the table while Rayna fumbled with the bottles a moment, trying to pop the tops with her left hand. Just when Wolf realized he should offer help since her right arm was still in the sling, she managed to win. She handed him one, sat down, and noticed he had a grin on his face.

"What?" she asked, suddenly self-conscious.

"Oh, nothing," he said, still smiling. "It's just that this is my favorite beer, and despite your injury, you opened it like a pro."

She nodded at the beer in his hand and ignored the teasing. "You have good taste."

Wolf returned the nod and took a piece of pizza. "So do you."

After a few bites in silent appreciation of the delicious meal, Rayna asked what he'd found at work that he had wanted to tell her about. Wolf swallowed and took a swig of his beer. "Oh, yeah. Right," he said and cleared his throat. "We went back into the caves today. Well, the rangers on duty were in there when I arrived. Way back in on one the dead-end passages, they found a package of items."

"Items?"

"Evidence, really," he answered. "It was in what kind of looked like a black zip-lock bag, the type used for water protection while camping or rafting. "He held up his hands about eighteen inches apart to give Rayna an idea of the size. "They said they found it sitting up in a crevice about seven feet off the ground. When they opened it, it took them a minute to figure out what they had." Wolf took another sip.

The suspense was killing Rayna. "Well?" He took a bite in response and she realized he was savoring her hanging on his every word as much as he was savoring that slice of pizza. "Your killing me here," she assured him.

"Sorry," he said between chews and pointed to the slice in his hand. "Good stuff." He finished that bite and picked up where he left off. "There were several maps of the area – road, topographical, property – all types. There were also full details of the nuclear plant up the river, including routes for transporting tritium rods down to South Carolina."

Rayna's jaw dropped. "You're kidding!"

"Nope! Not at all."

"Routes as in trucking routes?"

"Yes, and one that included a freight train, but mostly trucking."

Rayna let her mind wander for a minute. Maps and tritium transport routes, students of a supposed professor attending meetings about protesting the creation of more tritium, the group of students leaving the restaurant with Hampton and heading toward Bell Mountain... it was starting to come together. "Crap!" She snapped her fingers. "He was using the protests as cover!"

"What?"

"I bet the students, or at least some of them, were working with him."

Wolf gave her an intrigued look. "What students? Clearly, I've missed something here."

By the time Wolf left, it was after midnight. Rayna watched the Jeep back out of the driveway from her front door. Part of her had wanted Wolf to stay, but he had to work in the morning, she needed rest, and more importantly, she had no idea where their relationship was going. Every time she considered the thought that it might become more than friendship, she remembered Jess and how the woman had really just been convenient for him. Rayna had learned over the years not to fall into that trap. Convenience just covers up the loneliness for a short time until eventually, it actually increases it and leaves you feeling empty and stupid.

Their goodbye at the door had been on the verge of awkward. Both had been unsure of how to go about it. Wolf was afraid to hug her for fear of paining her arm. Rayna was afraid to assume he wanted a kiss. She never had been all that confident with men. She looked up into his intense blue eyes and went mum. Nothing smooth to say came to mind. In fact, her mind was just blank. His eyes were hypnotic. At the same time, he was staring down at her also saying nothing. What was he expecting? The best she could muster was "I guess I'll talk to you later?" He nodded, gave her a quick peck on the cheek, and walked away.

So, she stood just inside her door, watching his taillights disappear into the night, and questioned herself harshly over what she was doing. "Damn!" She whispered. Why wasn't dealing with a man ever easy? The only man in her life who had been predictable was Sam. Growing up together allowed her to know what made him tick, and she understood his habits, worries, fears, and humor. She'd never known any other guy as well as she knew Sam, which is why he was like the brother she never had. He watched out for her like a big brother should, too, and he knew her as well as she knew him.

She walked to her desk and looked at the computer's display. It was too late to call him, and she worried that a text might wake him. At the moment, she didn't trust email either. She was feeling more than a little paranoid over all computer-related communication after losing her laptop and her drive to God knows who.

Cloud stood in the office doorway and gave a low meow. Then the cat looked down the hall toward her bedroom. It was past their bedtime, and she knew it. Rayna shook her head and turned off the computer. "I know," she told the cat. "It's time for bed." Cloud nodded, flicked her tail in the air once, and ran for the bedroom.

Chapter 25

Fieldman was sitting at Sam's dining room table clicking an ink pen open and closed absently. It was late afternoon and the investigators had decided to have a quick meeting to discuss the report Moyra had emailed Sam earlier in the day. "It said what?" He clicked the pen again. The noise was irritating Rayna while she tried to process Sam's news.

"Results as expected," Sam repeated. He was standing, leaning against his kitchen counter.

Rayna sat at the little table opposite Fieldman, looking down at her hands folded in front of her. She hummed softly, thoughtfully.

"So, what does that mean?" Fieldman asked.

Sam shrugged. "Your guess is as good as mine. I mean I'm assuming it means that things worked, but…"

"But if they were expecting another leak, maybe they got it." Rayna finished for him.

Sam nodded. "Right." He paused. "Or it means nothing. Scientists like to say 'it worked' in as many ways as possible."

Rayna looked up at him sternly. "Correction – engineers do that. Scientists say 'more testing is required' because that's how they get paid."

Fieldman ignored the comment and clicked his pen again. "It sounds pretty cryptic to me."

Sam nodded in agreement.

"Maybe it's because someone knows we're looking?" Rayna suggested.

"It's not like we've been very quiet about it," Sam said. "I called every contact I had at the TVA and DOE."

Fieldman clicked his pen again, and Rayna reached across the table and gently pulled it from his hand. "Do you want some paper?" He asked.

"No thanks," she answered and set the pen down in front of her. The geologist looked confused. "I'm a little on edge without the pain meds this morning. Your clicking was about to drive me crazy."

"Oh, sorry." He said quietly and leaned back in his chair. "You didn't like the good stuff?"

Rayna knew he had some recreational drug use in his very distant past. Most of his generation did whether they admitted it or not. She had never approved, but never condemned it either. "I don't like taking anything that could become addictive. The doc said I'd only need it for a few days, so I only took it for two nights."

"So why are you edgy? Surely that wasn't enough to get you addicted." Fieldman said.

"My arm hurts, my head is starting to hurt, and I didn't get enough sleep, but I had too much coffee."

"Hmm… yeah…" He leaned forward. "Coffee's not addictive at all."

Rayna pursed her lips. She wasn't in the mood for sarcasm either, apparently.

Sam brought the conversation back to the subject at hand. "So what, if anything, do you think we should glean from this little tidbit?"

Rayna ran her hand through her hair. "I don't know. I think it means they've been testing, if nothing else. It's just too vague to make any other assumptions, though."

"I concur," Fieldman said.

Sam shrugged again. "Sorry guys. Weeks of digging and that's all I got."

Fieldman stood and put his hands in his pants pockets. "Well, since we've basically got nothing but a report that says not much more than nothing, I guess we're just stuck. This is so damned frustrating." He sighed.

Rayna shook her head. "It's not nothing. This is the first thing we've found that even acknowledges that testing was done in the past few months up there at the plant. It mentions tritium and a concern over leaks." She picked up the pen and tapped it on the table for emphasis. "That really is something. No, it's not a smoking gun, or an admittance to testing on farm animal corpses or an explanation for the hum or the UFO's, but it's another piece to our disjointed little puzzle, which means it's something."

"I guess," Fieldman said, but still sounded defeated. "I've got to get back to work. They'll eventually realize I'm not there when they need something from me."

Sam gave him a firm handshake. "Thanks for stopping by."

Rayna tossed Fieldman his pen. "I don't need it anymore," she said. "I'll see you later."

He clicked the pen closed and put it in his shirt pocket. "See ya," he said and then let himself out.

Sam sat down and rested his elbows on the table across from Rayna. "He was in a mood, wasn't he?"

"It seems like he's always in a mood lately," she answered. "The longer I know him the more I notice it, or the more cynical he becomes. I'm not sure which."

"At least we don't have to work with him on cases often. Ghosts and UFOs don't tend to intermingle much, and he's backed off doing paranormal investigations with us in the last year."

"Right," she agreed. "We don't deal with UFOs much. Well, really until now, we never have."

"I'm wondering if we're ever going to figure this one out. There are just too many missing pieces." Sam rested his chin on one palm. "We don't have any one direction right now."

"We know, or at least we suspect, that Hampton was using the caves and the students for cover while he apparently planned a tritium heist. That still may have some connection to the hum, since it's only been heard around Bell Mountain and the surrounding valleys, right?"

"Right."

"And we know that a number of people who don't seem to know each other have reported UFO sightings in recent months in the surrounding counties."

Again, Sam agreed.

"So, what about the idea that the aliens, or whatever, are interested in our nuclear power and our ability to make weapons of mass destruction? It's a popular theory… or hypothesis really."

"But how is Hampton connected to the UFOs?"

"I doubt he is or was. He was looking for a way to make money on a secret shipment of tritium from what we can tell. He just happened to show up around the same time as the UFOs, which just happened to show up at the same time that we believe the plant started making, or preparing to make, tritium rods. I really think we've got two separate puzzles here, or more like a Venn diagram with the plant being the only thing the two spheres have in common. In this case, it happens to be a big thing."

"So then, we really have extraterrestrials using our area as… what?"

Rayna shrugged. "Your guess is as good as mine. Hell! They could even be interdimensional beings for all we know."

"I'm not sure I care where they're coming from. I just want to know why they're here. If it's for research, what are they researching? If it's for abductions, why are they abducting? If they're here on vacation, did we put some intergalactic billboard out there in space somewhere?" He waved his hands wide as if to encompass the heavens.

She shook her head and smirked at her friend. "I wish I knew, but I doubt it was a billboard." She thought about it a moment and giggled.

"What?"

"I think the Eastern Tennessee Visitors Bureau has been holding out on us if they have that kind of funding." She pretended to be framing a large sign with her left hand. "Come to Jupiter! Not that one. The other one! See Earth's smallest wonder!"

Sam's mouth widened into a grin that highlighted his dimples. "Yeah... may not be the best hypothesis."

Chapter 26

Rayna struggled with the one-armed drive home from Sam's and decided the inventor of the automatic transmission was an unsung hero. As she put the truck in park in her driveway, her cell phone rang. "Hello, Ranger!" She answered with a little more enthusiasm than she would have liked to convey.

"Hello," he replied. "Are you terribly busy?"

"Not at all."

"Good! Then would you like to have dinner with me?"

Rayna's heart fluttered. "Yes," she answered as calmly as she could. "But," she added, "do you mind picking me up? I've had enough of driving for one day."

"Of course," he answered. I'll even drive you to a different town with a different diner, if you'd like."

The offer was sounding more like a lunch date by the second. "Oh, that sounds nice. Do you have any place in particular in mind?"

"No, but I'll think of something. I'm on my way." The phone clicked off.

Rayna exited the truck and was fumbling with her purse and the keys when her phone rang again. She answered without looking and dropped everything on the porch floor below her. She groaned a weak "hello."

"Miss Smith, this is Agent Black. I have some news for you."

"Hi, Agent Black. That's great! What do you have?" Rayna gave up on trying to get into her house and sat down on her porch step.

The agent cleared his throat on the other end of the call. "Former Agent Hampton has been processed and interrogated. We found your laptop and backup drive in his apartment, which has led to more questions with regard to what was on them."

"Uh-huh," Rayna wasn't sure how to reply. She had questions of her own, but feared demanding answers would get her nowhere. There was a brief silence, and her curiosity got the better of her. "Did he steal them for what was on them, or what he thought might be on them?"

"We believe he thought you knew more about his activities than you might be letting on."

"What activities?" Another long pause while she hoped for a straight answer. There was nothing, so she continued. "Do you mean how he created the humming sound near Bell Mountain? Or how he was going to use the student group he infiltrated to hijack a shipment of tritium rods?" If she was going to get anywhere, Rayna decided her best bet was to throw all their ideas about his involvement in the case out there. "What about the new waitress at the diner? She was involved, too, wasn't she?" Rayna honestly had no idea where that one came from. She was as surprised as Agent Black was to hear that question in her voice.

"How do you know about all of this?" Agent Black sounded a little perturbed.

"You're not the only investigator, Agent." She answered boldly. "I put things together pretty quickly when enough pieces to the puzzle surface."

"I see," he answered. "Yes, the new waitress at the diner was part of his student group. We arrested her this morning as an accomplice to Hampton. She is charged with kidnapping and larceny. We believe she helped attack your friend, drug him, and eventually drop him at the hospital in Knoxville – still unconscious."

"Oh, thank God!" Rayna let slip.

"I'm sorry?"

"I mean, we hoped his disappearance and reappearance were as mundane as that. His only memories of his kidnapping were pretty disturbing." She stopped herself short of mentioning alien abduction.

"I see." Agent Black took a deep breath. "What did you mean about the hum on Bell Mountain?"

"How did he create the sound Ranger Wolf has been searching for the source of? You know. The hum that's been reported in that area for the last several weeks?"

"We are not aware of those reports."

Rayna wondered if he was dodging answers again.

"Miss Smith, is that what you were researching on your laptop?"

"Partially, yes. I was also looking for the reason for the horse killing at an area farm. Do you know if Hampton had anything to do with that?"

"Can you describe it for me?"

Rayna wondered silently.if that was a trick question. *Oh, what the hell?* She'd said this much. She might as well keep going since she seemed to be getting somewhere. "The day before Lee was kidnapped, the Sheriff was called to the Lovell farm because somehow one of their horses had managed to fall *through* the tree tops. I mean – literally – dropped from above the trees. My paranormal investigation team was called in to add any insight we might have. One of our members is also a MUFON field investigator. I was researching why a farm animal might have been mutilated – and it was mutilated first – and then dropped on the same farm."

"Did you come to any conclusions?"

"After some soil testing, our best guess was that someone tested the animal for signs of tritium poisoning. We just couldn't figure out why they dropped the horse like that. It was pretty gruesome."

"That was apparently accidental." Agent Black answered. "Someone was transporting the horse via helicopter, and the cable broke. We're pretty sure the horse was deceased prior to its drop."

"Was it Hampton?"

"We think so, although, he hasn't fully admitted to it."

"What did he admit to?"

"I am not at liberty to say."

Rayna stamped the ground below her foot. "Then I guess we're done with our friendly conversation."

Black took another deep breath and a long pause followed. Rayna was about to hang up when he started talking again. "This is strictly off the record and between you and me, Miss Smith."

"Yes, sir."

"Agent Hampton was assigned to an undercover operation to investigate a student group whom we were told was planning to hijack a shipment of tritium and sell it on the black market. From what we can tell, he decided that the payday for such a sale would be worth risking his career, and he decided to lead the group. They were using Bell Mountain's caves as their base of operations. He stole your laptop and had one of the students steal your hard drive because he suspected you were on to him somehow."

"Then he shot me when I showed up in the cave because he thought I had tracked him there?"

"Yes. You were in the wrong place at the wrong time, but he thought it was by design."

"Sheesh!" Rayna flashed back to the fear she felt running through the caves away from the man with the gun. "We were just looking for the source of the hum."

"I'm still unsure what hum you're talking about. He didn't mention it."

Rayna's phone beeped to let her know another call was coming in. Reflexively, she looked at it. "I'm sorry, Agent. I think I really should answer this call. It's Mr. Lovell."

"I'll hold," was his short reply.

"Um… okay." Rayna clicked over. "Hello?"

The voice on the other end greeted her with a loud whisper. "Rayna?"

"Yes, this is Rayna."

"This Tim Lovell. Something is happening here. I think you should get down here."

"Tim, is everyone okay?"

"Yes," he whispered. "Please, just get here. I think you're going to want to witness this." Then his line went dead.

Rayna clicked back to Agent Black and tried to process her thoughts. "Are you still there?"

"Yes, I am."

"I'm sorry, Agent. I need to finish this conversation another time."

"Is there something I should know?"

"I have no idea," she answered honestly. "I will call you back later. I promise." With that, she hung up the phone. Just as she stood to gather herself and her things, Wolf pulled his Jeep into her driveway.

He saw her standing there with a puzzled expression, rolled down the window and asked, "What's wrong?"

"I don't know, but we have to get to the Lovell farm," she answered. "It sounded strange and urgent."

Chapter 27

Wolf's Jeep raced up the hilly driveway to the Lovell house. The sky was starting to change colors with the sun heading toward the western horizon. Rayna worried needlessly that it would soon be too dark to see what the family had called her out to witness. She hoped they didn't mind that she'd brought Wolf with her. If she needed an excuse, she could easily use her trouble driving with an injured arm.

The house looked deserted. Wolf parked close to the side porch, and the two exited the vehicle quickly. Wolf was making long, fast strides to the porch steps when Mrs. Lovell came springing around the side of the house from the backyard. "Back here!" She called in a loud whisper. "We're back here."

Wolf changed direction and passed Rayna in her effort to follow Sylvia. As she rounded the corner of the farmhouse, she saw the family standing near the picnic table, pointing back toward the woods. Shana caught Rayna's eye and put her index finger to pursed lips as if to say, "shh," and she pointed to her own right ear. Rayna stood still where she was and listened, her eyes rested on Wolf's face. In it, she saw a glimmer of recognition. At the same moment, her attention was drawn to a sound emanating from the woods at the edge of the yard. It was a hum of sorts, consistent and somewhat metallic and just loud enough to be heard over the sound of the house's HVAC system behind them.

Rayna walked slowly over to join the group and stood beside Wolf, facing the woods. She looked at his face and whispered, "You've heard this before."

He glanced at her in acknowledgement. "Yes," he replied quietly, "on the mountain the day before we met. Only it was louder."

"Do you hear it?" Tim Lovell asked them.

Rayna nodded. Wolf answered in the affirmative.

"It's been almost 90 minutes since it started," the farmer said.

"Have you been back there?" Wolf asked.

"The missus won't let me," Tim answered. "Not after the horse incident. That's why I called you."

Wolf looked at Rayna expectantly. She imagined she knew what his eyes were asking. She took a deep breath and glanced back toward the woods. There was really only one way to find out what the source of the noise was. "Do you have your gun?" she asked him. He answered with a single nod and tapped the holster strapped to his belt. Rayna wasn't really sure if it helped her to know Wolf was armed, but at least she thought to ask this time. She gave the ranger a half-grin. "Right. Okay, then," she pointed at the woods. "Shall we?"

Wolf nodded again and then turned to the Lovells who were watching them intently. "Call the Sheriff and stay here." Tim, Sylvia, and Shana nodded simultaneously. The pair didn't wait to see each of them pull their cell phones out at the same time. Instead, they focused on the wood line and walked cautiously toward it.

With the sun setting, behind them, the woods were already darkening. The tall pine trees threw long shadows across the forest floor. Everything seemed to have been painted in muted browns and mossy greens and splattered with a growing stain of blackness.

Wolf and Rayna paused just inside the tree line to let their eyes adjust to the heavily filtered, waning daylight. In her rush to get to the farm, she realized now that she had not thought to grab a flashlight. In fact, her go-bag was sitting behind the bench seat of her truck in her driveway. She suddenly felt naked. She had nothing but her own senses to go on. Wolf moved beside her. That was right, she reminded herself. She wasn't alone, and Rayna couldn't think of anyone else she'd rather have beside her at that moment. The motion he had made while she was lost in thought was that of a well-trained ranger quietly drawing his handgun out of its holster. He held it with both hands, lowered in front of him.

Once Rayna's eyes were adjusted, she focused on her other senses. She could still hear the hum, which seemed louder. She also noticed an absence of other sounds. There were no birds singing, squirrels scrambling, crickets chirping, or any other noise you'd expect in the woods at dusk. Everything was still – extremely still. She motioned to Wolf to listen. He mouthed the words "too quiet" to her. Somehow – just like in the movies – the animals always know when there is an odd presence in the woods. Rayna guessed they could feel the vibration associated with the increasingly loud humming. It was getting louder, wasn't it? "Louder or closer?" she wondered.

Wolf motioned to her that he was ready to move forward by lifting his chin and directing his eyes ahead. Rayna took a step to her left, a little closer to him and his gun before nodding her agreement. They crept a few steps forward together. What happened next froze them in their tracks. The hum abruptly ceased.

Within a few seconds, beyond the trees in front of them, they saw a flash of brilliant yellow light. Although it was only seen through the branches and tree trunks, it was so incredibly bright that both Rayna and Wolf were momentarily blinded. They stood like the proverbial deer in headlights, frozen in the silence.

Rayna felt like it took forever to blink away the brightness and be able to focus in the shadows again. Wolf, blinking too, looked at her and whispered, "What the hell?"

Rayna didn't have an answer. She was still processing what her eyes thought they were seeing in front of her: movement in the trees ahead of them. "Do you see what I'm seeing?" she didn't look to see if Wolf nodded. Instead, she stayed focused on making out the motion, if there really was any there. The longer she stared, the more she began to question if she was just looking at the effects of a subtle breeze through the low-hanging branches. The situation seemed eerily familiar to her.

Wolf's answer didn't help her decide. "I don't know." She finally broke her gaze to glance at him. He returned the glance and shrugged. "I'm still seeing spots."

A small sound, like a snapping twig in the woods made both of them jerk their eyes back to those trees. Rayna held her breath. Wolf raised his gun a little higher. There was another, brief, smaller flash of light from behind the trees. This time, it was more like a neon green flashlight beam. Only, it seemed to come from above the trees and down through the branches aiming toward the ground about ten feet in front of them. Rayna blinked, and it was gone.

The next flash came from a different angle, but still above the trees. It illuminated the ground five or six feet to Wolf's left side. Rayna pointed around him, and in the time it took for him to turn his head, it was gone. The next flash hit directly to her right and turned the grass by her foot an eerie color. She instinctively jumped to her left, right into Wolf's side. He had turned toward the flash just in time to see her jump and catch her with his right arm, his gun in his left hand then. He steadied her, and Rayna felt a tinge of embarrassment that she had flinched, as well as a little pain in her injured arm.

All was dark again. She was sure she heard movement through the woods in front of them. It was starting to look as if the tree trunks were moving.

Sudden motion behind them made Wolf turn quickly, gun raised and ready to shoot. "Wait!" a familiar voice hissed. "Wait. FBI."

Rayna turned briefly from the specter in the forest to see the same two agents who had escorted her from the emergency room.

"What are you doing here? Where's the Sheriff?" She asked in a loud whisper, turning her attention back to the woods.

"What the hell?" Wolf said again.

"Shit!" Agent Black gasped.

The moving tree trunks no longer looked like tree trunks. They were approaching... *beings*.

Rayna had never felt fear like this before. Her heartbeat was pounding in her ears. Her breathing was quick and shallow, and she felt like she was trapped in a nightmare. Her eyes, she hoped, must be deceiving her. Too many "X-files" episodes, she tried to tell herself. They were coming back and playing tricks on her mind. Disbelief filtered in and fought back the terror. Her investigative instincts started questioning everything as quickly as her mind could process the unfolding scene.

These creatures, walking ever so slowly toward them were barely more than stick figures – thin, gray, and spectral. The shadows of the trees made discerning their facial features difficult. She was afraid to look too closely, though. She had an idea of what she might see, and the idea was too creepy for her. Instead, she focused on their movement. It was slow and deliberate. They were getting closer to the four, but not by normal ambulatory motion. These beings were definitely humanoid – two arms, two legs, hands, feet, torso, oddly long neck, large heads, and… "don't look at the eyes," she told herself. They should have been walking on those two spindly legs, but they weren't really. They were gliding. Unnervingly and unrealistically gliding.

Rayna wondered why Wolf hadn't moved to fire his gun, or at least give warning that he would. Then, she realized that he wasn't moving at all, and neither were the agents behind them. All four seemed frozen in place. Rayna briefly questioned if she would be able to move. She fought the fear of being immobilized and tried to make a subtle motion, so as not to alert the entities closing the distance between them. Rayna focused on her right arm, still in that stupid, beige sling, and wiggled her thumb. She felt it respond to her mental command. Now the question was *should* she move and not whether she could.

A voice in her head said, "Be not afraid." It was not her own inner voice, nor that of anyone she'd heard before. She remembered her favorite church hymn from her childhood. A sense of calm serenity washed over her. She felt peaceful instead of fearful, and she wondered if her guardian angel had spoken the words. Even with her fear abated, she still stood frozen in time.

She blinked and realized that one of the creatures was now in front of her, within her personal space. It was taller than the typical gray aliens that she'd read about in so many reports. Rayna stood five-and-a-half feet tall, and this one was eye-to-eye with her. Eye-to-eye. She had no choice but to look at those big, dark eyes. She didn't know what to expect, but the result was less than whatever she might have imagined. Those eyes were black like coal, almond shaped, and empty. They held no expression and no impression. They were just there. She felt nothing from looking at them. Clearly, alien eyes were not the windows to their souls like human eyes were. There was no sense of hypnosis or trance induction. There was precisely nothing.

How odd that the one encounter that she had feared most for her entire life – or at least, since realizing there was possibly of such a thing as aliens at a young age – was the one encounter that cancelled any sense of fear that she had at the beginning! It was one of the most neutral feelings she'd ever experienced. She turned her head slowly to look at Wolf to her left. He was staring blankly at the being in front of him. His gun in his left hand hung limply at his side. He seemed to feel her eyes on him and without looking away from the gray figure asked, "What do they want?"

One of the agents behind Rayna whispered, "I don't know."

Rayna looked back to the being standing in front of her and summoned the words, "Can I help you?" She wasn't sure what answer she expected, but she heard nothing in response. Of course, she didn't really think that aliens from another planet or dimension or whatever would speak English. The figure raised a thin, willowy hand slowly, as if it were being cautious. Beside her, Rayna sensed Wolf direct his attention toward her and the visitor in front of her. His energy shifted from neutral – as hers remained – to protective. She didn't move, but said quietly, "It's okay, Wolf."

He stayed still, and she felt him relax a little. The alien tilted its head forward and down, an odd motion that looked as if its oversized head should snap off of its tiny neck and roll away. It seemed to be examining her slinged arm. The creature settled its lifted hand gently on the outward facing part of the sling. A quick surge of energy rushed through Rayna's arm from fingers to shoulder and then radiated out across her body. It wasn't painful, but it was sudden and unexpected. Rayna recognized the subtle sensation the energy left when it subsided. It was like Reiki – a healing use of life energy she had once learned long ago. The feeling of peacefulness returned to her, and the alien lifted its slender hand and glided back just a bit.

"Are you okay?" Wolf whispered, still unmoving.

"Yes," Rayna answered. Reflexively, she wiggled her fingers and rolled her right shoulder. In the process, she noted that the back of her arm didn't sting with the usual twinge of pain. She lifted her right shoulder again, and encouraged by the continued lack of pain, straightened her arm as much as she could with the sling still in place. There was still no pain. She smiled a closed-mouth smile at the being. "Thank you," she whispered.

The beings turned after a moment of silence and retreated back into the dark woods. The four investigators stayed motionless, watching the visitors fade back into the landscape. There was another blinding flash of light and the world was completely silent.

Agent Black broke the stillness. "What the hell just happened?"

To Rayna, it seemed obvious. They'd just had a very close encounter. She wondered if the guy had blacked out. Before she could respond, Wolf turned to her and gently touched her shoulders. "What did it do to you?" He asked quietly.

Rayna looked down at her sling. There seemed to be a slight discoloration where the being had touched it, and to her surprise, it was faintly glowing. "I'm not totally sure," she answered. She lifted the back of the sling and pulled it up and over her head and slipped her arm out of it. She twisted to try to get a look at the back of her arm, but it was too difficult. She wished she had a mirror.

Wolf walked around beside her and touched her elbow gently. "It's hard to tell in the darkness. We should probably go find some light before we lift the bandage to look at it."

Rayna nodding in agreement, slowly straightened her arm. She still expected some pain caused by moving her tricep, but she felt nothing. She smiled.

"What the hell just happened?" Black repeated louder.

Rayna turned her attention to him and Agent Holmes. "I think they just helped me."

"What?" asked Holmes.

Rayna moved her arm again. Still no pain. "I'll be interested to see what it looks like now." She and Wolf started walking toward the Lovell's farm house. The two FBI agents just stood there, looking back into the darkened woods. Rayna paused and said, "They're not there, guys."

Wolf kept moving and whispered to her, "I wonder if they're going to report this."

Rayna shrugged and caught up to him. "I know if they don't, then I won't. What about you?"

"What happens in my free time does not get put into a report." Wolf answered with a sideways grin.

Sheriff Sutton and five deputies were standing halfway between the Lovells' back patio and the tree line, flashlights in their hands, watching Rayna and Wolf cross the yard. "What happened?" Dean asked when they were within ten feet of each other.

"What did you see?" Rayna answered a question with a question.

"What we heard," the sheriff answered, "was that infamous hum. Other than two God-awfully bright flashes through the trees, we didn't see anything."

"Really?" Rayna was surprised. "I thought for sure you'd see the craft from out here."

"Craft?" Dean looked puzzled.

"Craft." Wolf repeated. "I think you could say we just had a close encounter of… some kind."

The deputies just stared. Shana Lovell stepped out from behind them and pointed to the sling in Rayna's left hand. "Are you okay?"

Rayna looked down at it and then over her right shoulder toward the injured tricep. "I think so. Can we use your bathroom for a moment?"

One of the deputies laughed harshly. "Why? D'ya piss yer pants?" His accent was thick. Rayna did not look to see who had spoken.

Wolf scowled. "I didn't see you in those woods, Deputy." The man lowered his gaze to his feet. "Sheriff, there are two federal agents still in those woods. They seemed okay, but you might want to check on them if they don't come out soon."

Wolf and Rayna followed Shana inside the farm house. The bathroom was bright with a large mirror over the vanity. Shana stood back while Wolf helped Rayna slip off the bandages. The skin underneath was whiter than the rest of her arm. She angled herself in the mirror so that she could see the back of it. Wolf stared in disbelief, and Rayna felt a warmth permeate her body.

"Didn't you just get shot like a week ago?" Shana's voice filled the room.

Rayna looked at the teenager and nodded. "Less than a week, actually."

"In your arm?"

"Yes," Rayna answered and pointed at her unbandaged tricep. "Right here. The bullet took a chunk of tissue with it."

Shana gasped. "I don't see a mark!"

"Amazing," Wolf finally said.

Rayna turned her attention to her arm in the mirror again. "Indeed."

Epilogue

James Fieldman was clicking his pen again. This time, it was between questions as he made notes on Rayna's statement about her encounter. The man was irritated.

"Come on," Rayna pleaded. "Don't be mad. All Tim said was that I needed to come to the farm. He didn't say, 'come to the farm so you can have a close encounter.' I would have totally called you if he did."

They sat in a booth with Sam and Wolf at a Chinese buffet in a little town about 30 minutes from Jupiter. Wolf and Rayna's dinner date had become a debriefing. She'd lost hope for a romantic dinner at the farm when they decided to call Sam and Fieldman to tell them what happened. Fieldman insisted she make a report to MUFON even if she did it somewhat anonymously. While she told her story, he grew fidgety. Jealous. Rayna knew he'd wanted that kind of experience for himself, but she couldn't give it to him. She would have, but she couldn't.

Sam changed the subject. "Can we get back to what that FBI agent told you? Did he say if Hampton mentioned seeing a UFO? I mean... he had the same sort of sunburn that Lee had, right? And when do you get your computer stuff back?"

"Agent Black seemed truly oblivious to any UFO reports and the humming sound we were investigating. Although, you know I do think Hampton and that young waitress just happened to see what made that triangular shape near Lee's car. I bet it all happened when they were moving him and emptying the trunk. All that makeup she was wearing could have hidden burn marks like theirs." Rayna had thought of that on the way to dinner. "Anyway, he said he would bring my stuff to me by the end of the week."

"Do you think it will be wiped clean?" Fieldman was always the suspicious one.

"Why would they do that? Everything related to the case was either from public domain websites, or the soil sample report, which I would still have access to through Vincent."

He clicked his pen again. "I guess." Rayna reached for the pen and he put it on the table for her. "Sorry. Maybe I am a little envious of your experience this evening."

"I know," she said soothingly. "I'm sorry you weren't there." Then she looked at Wolf and added, "but I'm glad Wolf was."

He smiled, and it lit up her world. "I wouldn't have missed it," he told her.

Sam cleared his throat. "Why didn't you take a shot at those creepy aliens?"

"Why should I have?" Wolf asked. "They were creepy, but not threatening. What might they have done if I did? Certainly, Rayna's arm would still be injured, or worse. If they have that kind of control over energy for healing, what other things can they do with it?"

"I guess that makes sense," Sam said thoughtfully. He turned his attention to his best friend of decades. "So, young lady, what's next for you?"

Rayna was puzzled. "What do you mean? Like dessert?"

He laughed. "Maybe icing on the cake, yeah," he said and nodded toward Wolf.

She blushed. "I have no idea what you mean!"

Wolf did. "Maybe, Rayna, you might consider having dinner with me tomorrow evening? Just the two of us?"

She blushed again. "I would like that very much."

And just like that her life wasn't about filling time to avoid lonesomeness; it was about spending time with someone she truly enjoyed being near.

The Tritium Hypothesis

Biography

Nicolle Morock lives in the Triangle area of North Carolina and works in meteorology, digital media, concert production, and whatever else strikes her fancy. Her hobbies include paranormal investigation and research. Her roommate is Penny, a black cat who keeps odd hours and makes sure Nicolle takes time to play.

Photo credit: Nelson Nauss

The Tritium Hypothesis

Made in the USA
Columbia, SC
16 April 2019